Praise for *On The Edge,* the first Cole Buckman novel

"An intense, powerful page turner."

—Linda Power

"Absolutely loved this book! A perfect balance of adventure and substance. Honestly, I felt like I was watching a spy movie in my mind, as I was reading it. I also thoroughly enjoyed how it left me feeling content that the current adventure had been completed, but teasing me that there's more to come."

—Sarah Wilson

"Grabs you from the beginning and won't let you go!"

—Steve B

"*On the Edge* is a great read. The key characters are well developed early in the book. The story moves along briskly and has some interesting twists as it progresses. A good story well told. "

— Steve Cavell

SHADOW MAN

A COLE BUCKMAN NOVEL

Written by Marina L. Reed

with Don Hawkins

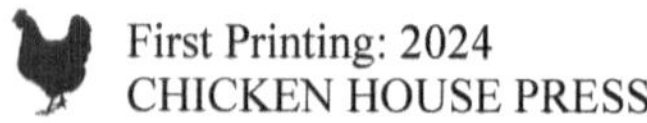 First Printing: 2024
CHICKEN HOUSE PRESS

Library and Archives Canada Cataloguing in Publication
CIP data on file with the National Library and Archives

ISBN trade paperback edition: 978-1-990336-84-3

Chicken House Press
282906 Normanby/Bentinck Townline
Durham, Ontario, Canada, N0G 1R0

www.chickenhousepress.ca

Cover art by J. Mitchel Reed and Alanna Rusnak

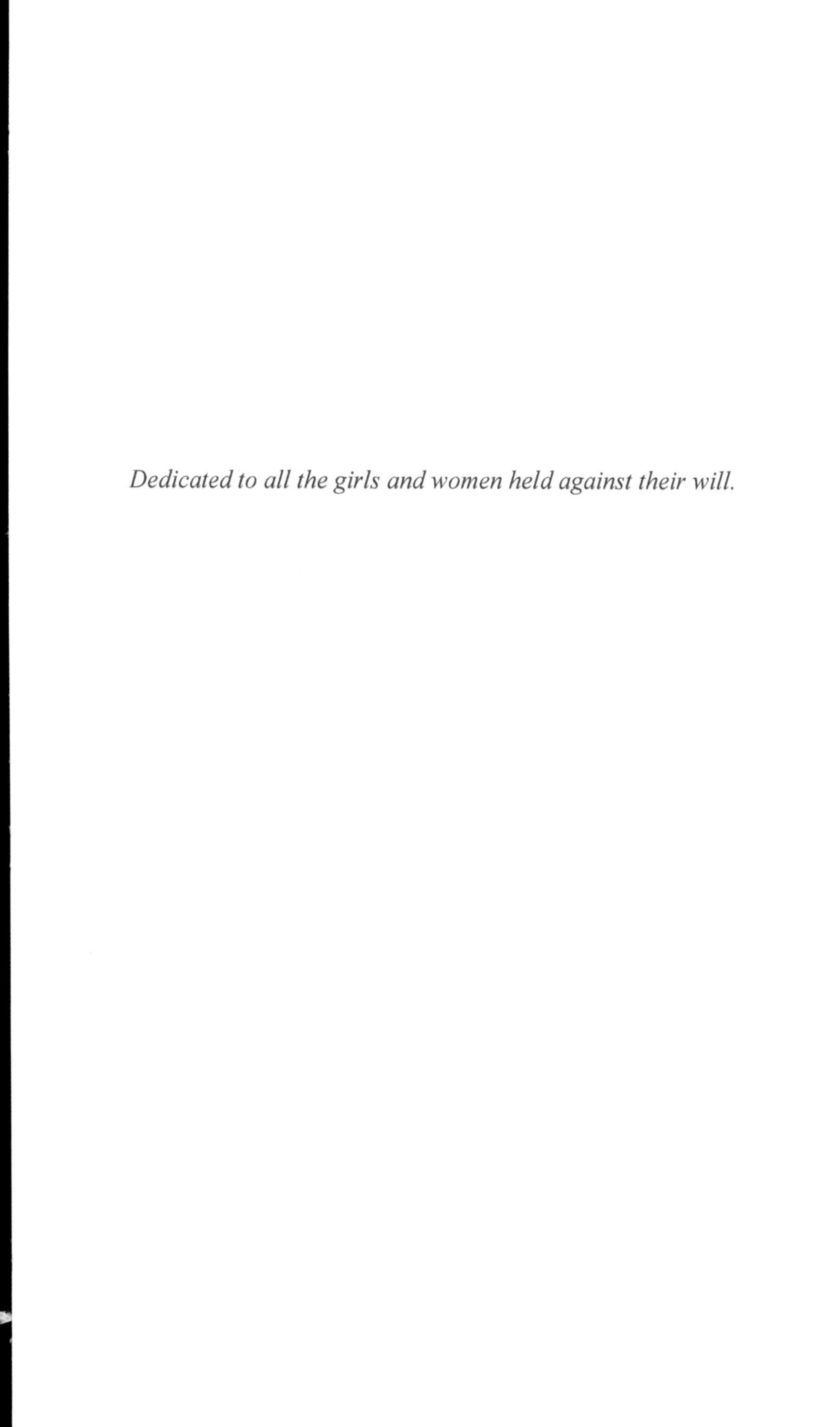

Dedicated to all the girls and women held against their will.

Other Books by Marina L. Reed

<u>Fiction</u>
On the Edge: A Cole Buckman Novel (1)
Primrose Street
It's Lonely in Paradise
No, You Wouldn't

Coming soon...
Death at the Yellow Briar: A Cole Buckman Novel (3)

<u>Non-Fiction</u>
A new paradigm for grief series
  Remember, It's OK: Loss of a Parent
  Remember, It's OK: Loss of a Partner
  Remember, It's OK: Loss of a Sibling/Friend
  Remember, It's OK: Loss of a Child
  Remember, It's OK: Loss of a Pet
  Remember, It's OK: Loss for Teens
Jayne's INpowered Handbook

SHADOW MAN

Marina L. Reed
with Don Hawkins

BUENOS AIRES | ARGENTINA | 2016

The cab pulled up to the front door of the Hilton Hotel in Buenos Aires. Cole Buckman paid in cash and stepped cautiously into the warm night air, scanning the area. The pocket of his jeans held the keycard for room 812. He walked by the front desk to the elevator, stepped inside the waiting open doors, put on his gloves, and pushed the button for the seventh floor. Elevator music filled the cubicle. He leaned against the wall, folding his arms across his chest, watching the lights change to different numbers on the panel. Number seven lit up, and he stepped forward as the bell alerted him to the doors opening. He exited the elevator, found the stairs, and took them two at a time to the next floor up. He walked down the hall to room 812, inserted the keycard to open the door, and stepped inside. The assistant director of the Secret Intelligence Service, MI6, Patricia Ivy, a.k.a. Poison Ivy, had made sure the HK45 Compact Tactical handgun would be secured in the room's safe when Cole arrived. He punched the code he'd been given onto the keypad …12372… and pulled out the weapon that had waited coldly, alone in the dark chamber. He cradled it in his hands for a moment; it was every hit-man's dream tool—optics-ready slide, suppressor height sights, threaded barrel, silencer.

Cole's mission was to eliminate MI6 agent Ted

Harper. Buckman knew Harper. They had trained together in the early days, having been recruited simultaneously. In the years that followed, they had executed missions together. They had been a good team. Now Intel had assessed Harper as a double agent currently aligned with a South American drug cartel; it was discovered that he'd been profiting from MI6 missions for years. The information came as a shock to Cole. He liked Harper. There had been trust working together. He never thought he'd be asked to use his skills against him. But a mission was a mission. The moment he started to question that—if he started bringing emotion into the job; if he started second-guessing directives—he would be the one with a bullet in the back of his head. Cole knew too much, and he became a liability the minute he blinked a hesitation, a question to authority. When Poison assigned you a mission, no questions were tolerated. He pushed his emotions to a back corner of his mind. Emotions had to die or he did, so he focused on the job, just the job.

Cole's outfit was laid out on the bed: black dress slacks, black golf shirt, black sports jacket. He dressed quickly, tucked his handgun into his waistband, covered it with his jacket, and then secured the Fairbairn-Dykes fighting knife his grandfather had given him years ago into the holster on his lower right leg. That knife had got him out of a lot of dicey situations; it was his secret weapon, sometimes literally. It was like another appendage.

The clothes he'd been wearing when he first entered room 812 were left on the bathroom floor; the agency's cleanup crew would dispose of them within the hour. He stepped into the hall, glanced from left to right, checked for time, and checked the safety on his watch, where an explosive was hidden in case he needed a quick exit strategy.

He didn't have time to wait for an elevator, instead opting for the stairs. He made his way to the pool. Just before 10:00 p.m., Harper was scheduled to arrive for his nightly swim. He was a very deliberate man. He always did the same lengths of the pool at the same hour of the day. With Harper in the water, it was otherwise empty on the deck, except for a waiter walking toward a poolside table with a tray of drinks, clearly for after Harper's swim. Time was ticking. With panther-like stealth, Cole moved behind the waiter, covered his mouth with his gloved hand, and applied Dim Mak to his neck, rendering him instantly unconscious. He caught the slumped body in one arm and the tray in the other, lowered the body to the ground. He placed the tray on the table with not a drop spilled from a glass. He would wake up when Cole had left, not remembering a thing.

Cole often used Dim Mak from his black belt training.

It was quick, instant and painless, smooth and fluid, like a barracuda in its element. In the wrong hands it could cause death, but Cole's were never the wrong hands.

Cole stepped over the body and walked toward the pool, staying in the shadows, waiting for the moment. Harper swam to the side of the pool, and his hands reached up to the ledge. His head went down as he hoisted himself out of the pool. Cole emerged from the shadows. As Harper uncurled himself to a standing position, water glistening and dripping off his skin, his head came up, face-to-face with Cole and his weapon. Harper's face instantly drained of blood. There was a flash of recognition and possibly regret before Cole double-tapped him in the chest and then put a bullet in the middle of his forehead. Harper's body fell back into the pool, his blood mingling with the chlorinated water.

Cole secured his weapon, rapidly collected the three shell casings, and disappeared.

BALZAC'S, THE DISTILLERY, TORONTO, ONTARIO, CANADA, 2016

Bill Thornton walked over to the table carrying two cups of coffee and two pastries. He put them down on the table, and Trish Anderson smiled.

"That was pretty impressive," she said.

"What?"

"Getting all that stuff to the table without anything crashing to the floor," she said.

"Oh, that." Bill smiled sideways. "You didn't know I was with Cirque du Soleil for a while?"

"You're kidding, right?"

"Of course I'm kidding." He snickered.

"I wouldn't put anything beyond you, my friend. You have done a lot of weird shit undercover."

"Well, that is true, but swinging around on a thin wire hundreds of feet in the air… not happening." He sat down.

"Why is the coffee so good here?" she cooed.

"Probably because it's 8:00 a.m., and it's your first cup."

She laughed. "Yeah, maybe." She took another long sip. "This is nice, having a coffee like this. We never get a chance when we're involved in a case."

"Yeah, true. But we used to always come here way back when."

"I remember. We were both babies on the police force then."

"Well, *you* were the baby."

"Okay, I was the baby. You were a toddler."

"You're right, though, we should do this more often. It is good to get out."

"We needed a break too. The last case was pretty intense." She sipped her coffee and took another piece off her pastry.

"It was, but they all are."

"Which is why we keep coming back for more. Speaking of which, when is Cole back?"

"I don't know. He's on some secret mission." Bill rolled his eyes.

"Isn't he supposed to be doing all those with us now?"

"He still does the occasional work for the agency. Keeps him sharp, I guess. Heard from him?" He dug into his pastry.

"I did, actually. He said Mac had messaged him about the daughter of a colleague that had gone missing."

"When are Mac and Cole going to finally tie the knot?"

"Probably never, but they've got a good thing going. No need to rock the boat." Trish swallowed her mouthful of pastry and took another sip of coffee. "What colleague do you think Cole was talking about?"

"Mac has a lot of those, but she's pretty close to Jim Morrison. They served together, and he has two daughters."

"Okay, that makes sense. Do you think it's serious?

That she's missing?" Trish asked.

"I'd give it a few days at least. Teenagers are always pulling shit like that."

"How do you know? You don't have any."

"Not for lack of trying."

Trish smiled and punched him on the shoulder. "No, seriously, does he have a reason to worry?"

"They could just be at a friend's house, phones on Do Not Disturb."

"I'm pretty sure teen girls will never have their phones muted; it's their lifeline. But true, there could be lots of reasons."

"I'm sure they will be in contact pretty soon."

"Girls are always at risk now," Trish asked.

"More at risk than before?"

"I'm gonna say yes." She polished off the last piece of pastry. "Fuck, that pastry tasted like another." She laughed, lifting her coffee to her lips.

"Why do you say 'yes' like that?" Bill said.

"I was talking to someone I worked with on the force the other day. We keep in touch. He was saying there is a lot more trafficking of girls than ever before. And not just girls from overseas. Girls in our own backyards. Apparently they were getting close to pulling in a local crime syndicate trafficking girls, they had everything lined up, and one of their newer cops…"

"How new?"

"Couple of years on the force, I think. Anyway, she gave them the wrong info, so the cops were at the wrong place at the wrong time and they missed their chance."

"Fuck. Seriously? That's shit. Is she still on the force?"

"Yeah, she is. Got a slap on the wrist, that was it. But these were local girls, around Kingston, I think. So it really stung. So much time was put into that op."

"That's tough. She must know someone high up. Who was the cop who fucked up?"

"I think her name was Stokely."

"Doesn't ring a bell. Cops can't afford mistakes like that. Not these days. And you're right, trafficking is getting bigger. There are girls being sold all over Ontario for big money."

"Border towns like Niagara Falls and Kingston are big players."

"Toronto too."

"Yeah, what a fucking mess. Makes me sick. Who are these people selling girls? I'd hate to have a daughter out there these days. Hope that guy's daughter turns up soon."

"Me too."

"Hey Bill, how about another Cirque du Soleil act! I could really go for another round."

"Naw, it's your turn."

"Okay, if you want to be eating off the floor, no problem at all." Trish pushed her seat back to get up, but Bill beat her to it, and put a hand on her shoulder.

"I'll do it. I'm not a fan of floor cuisine. Maybe check in with Cole."

"Will do. We should be all meeting together soon. There's bound to be something he wants us to do."

"Isn't there always?"

"Keeps us young," Trish said.

"Speak for yourself."

"I am," said Trish, smiling.

NIAGARA FALLS, ONTARIO, CANADA

It was Hailey Morrison's sixteenth birthday, and she was getting out of her hick town. At least for a few days. The weekend, to be more precise. Her dad was away, as usual, for work; her grandparents wouldn't suspect a thing. She told them she'd be having a sleepover with her besties. So easy. She and her friends, Maddie and Nina, had been planning it for months, watching TikTok videos about ways to have a getaway, videos of clubbing fun, feeling much older than 16 and wanting a taste of the big city, all on their own, on their terms. They knew they were ready. They had acquired their fake IDs from a friend of a friend of a friend, booked a room at a hotel in Niagara Falls, Ontario, and had their bus tickets in their iPhone wallets. They had been saving allowance and part-time job salaries for months. They'd gone shopping to buy just the right outfits for nightclubbing, having googled the hell out of it, as well as handbags, short skirts, high heels, and lots of bling. They'd researched different hairstyles and makeup to ensure they resembled their fake ID ages. Everything was packed in their knapsacks so they didn't attract too much attention. On the bus, they'd tell people they were going to visit relatives, if anyone asked. But people rarely talked to chattering groups of aloof hormonal teenagers. They figured they'd be left alone. Plus, they didn't look 12 years old or like they were running away. Because, well, they weren't. Just a girls' weekend.

They told Nina's mom they were going to the mall. A normal activity for a Saturday afternoon. They smiled. Waved. Moved quickly, so no questions could be asked. Nina's mom smiled and waved. She realized there was little she could say. That had become apparent when her daughter turned 14. "See you for dinner," Nina's mom called out.

"Unless we just grab a pizza. We'll text," said Nina. And the door slammed behind them. Nina's mother shook her head and walked into the kitchen.

The girls giggled as they made their way to the bus terminal, picking up a Tim Hortons coffee as they went. It was all so smooth and easy. They settled into the seat at the back of the bus, backpacks on the floor between their feet, phones in right hand, coffee in their left.

Hailey's grandparents were a bit disappointed she wouldn't be home for her birthday. Grammy Morrison had made her favourite chocolate cake with sprinkles, topped with sixteen sparkler candles. That was for after their special dinner out; reservations had been made at Chez Renee. They had also organized a FaceTime with her dad, Jim Morrison, as a surprise. He was on a mission in the Middle East. Getting that set up was no small feat, but Grammy was a determined woman. All that would now have to be cancelled. Hailey had just announced she wouldn't be home for her birthday. And when they tried to say anything, there was the standard speech from Hailey about how it was her life, she wasn't a baby anymore, and so on. Grammy could almost recite it as the words came out of Hailey's mouth. Abby, her older sister, had been different. She had always been more settled, happy to be home and study. She was at Trent University studying political science. Grammy had thought of calling her and asking her to intervene. But she couldn't always be doing that. It wasn't Abby's place. So she just left it. She sent Hailey a happy birthday text that morning, getting no reply.

The girls peered out the windows of the bus as tall hotels began to pop up in the distance. When they exited at the bus at the terminal, they stopped, looking up and around, breathing in the city smell of energy, concrete, exhaust fumes, baked goods, and freedom. They hailed a cab, as they'd seen in countless movies, and all piled into the back seat.

"Falls Lodge, please," Hailey told the cab driver in a very authoritative voice she'd learned from her dad. The other girls stifled their giggles, their eyes wide with melodrama. They checked into the lodge a little after 7:00 p.m. using their phoney IDs and nonchalantly walked down the hall to their room on the first floor: 138. They turned the keycard over a few times until it finally fit properly in the slot and the little green light flicked on. They all looked quickly at each other, smiles creeping onto their cheeks, and opened the door. Once inside, they collapsed on the beds in fits of laughter, nervous tension, and over-the-moon excitement.

They hadn't told anyone where they were going.

MILITARY BASE, TRENTON, ONTARIO, CANADA

Navy Lieutenant Mackenzie Gallo adjusted her laptop on the small pullout tray in front of her as the CC-144 Challenger sped her back to Ontario. She sipped at her ginger ale. Being a member of the elite Special Intelligence Branch (a highly covert Canadian Joint Army, Navy, and Airforce group) allowed her to move around the world with no questions asked. On this trip home she was able to catch a ride with diplomats heading back to Canada after meetings in Britain. Mac Gallo was involved in a military case overseas, but after she received a coded email from Major James Morrison, she knew she had to get back to Canada ASAP. She had said she had an urgent intelligence meeting at Parliament Hill, and no one questioned her. It was a quiet flight, with every passenger engaged in their own business within their own technology. She opened her laptop and clicked on the coded email. Jim Morrison was currently on a covert operation in the Middle East. The only reason he would be communicating outside his mission and in code to Mac was if he thought something was wrong. Since his wife died, Mac had been getting messages like this more and more. This message said that he'd received word his daughter Hailey hadn't come home for a few days, and he was asking Mac to see what was going on.

Mac knew she owed her life to Jim. She turned her gaze to the small oval window beside her, the clouds drifting her mind back to that mission in Turkey years ago; she still couldn't believe how it had all gone so wrong so quickly…

It had been early-morning hours in Istanbul. Clouds dotting an otherwise pearl-blue sky provided the backdrop for the coup currently underway in the country. It was chaos. Soldiers and tanks crawled through the streets, and explosions rang out in Ankara and Istanbul. Turkish fighter jets dropped bombs on their own parliament in Ankara, and the chairman of the joint chiefs of staff was kidnapped by his own security.

At 7:00 a.m., Mac and Jim entered the Istanbul Airport, waiting for their flight to Britain. They looked like civilians in their beige khaki pants and dark blue t-shirts rather than agents on a mission. While waiting, they saw Sarah James, executive assistant to the Canadian ambassador, standing by a vending machine, her face as white as the floor tiles. Upon seeing them, she ran over, distraught. She quickly explained that the Canadian ambassador, Woodward, had been on a yacht with the Turkish president when the coup broke out. He was in danger. A military chopper had been sent to lift the Turkish president to safety, but only the president. Word had it that rebels were waiting for the yacht to dock in Gocek and would take everyone prisoner. Sarah had already called Ottawa but was told they could not get involved. Jim had given Mac that "look." She knew the look well; it always meant they would be doing something off the books, off off off the books. She pursed her lips. Off the books during a coup was a dangerous option. But she knew when Jim gave that "look," he'd made his mind up. She had two choices: leave or stay. She stayed. Never leave a man behind, or alone.

Jim made calls. It was arranged. A military-prepped Jeep Grand Cherokee was waiting outside the airport. Their new mission was the extraction of the Canadian ambassador before he could be taken by the rebels.

As Mac and Jim approached Gocek in the Jeep with the MP5 machine gun under the passenger seat, rebels seemed to be everywhere. They were checking vehicles coming and going, and boats in the harbour. Mac parked and waited, her Browning Hi-Power pistol on alert in her holster. Jim sauntered into the marina, casually smoking a Marlboro, his Browning handgun in the back of his pants, hidden under his t-shirt. He watched the yacht maneuver into a slip. Immediately, there was a flurry of people, on and off the boat, guns waving, intensity high. The ambassador stepped off the ship and amidst the chaos, Jim grabbed him. They ran for the Jeep in a flurry of gunfire.

Mac gripped the steering wheel as the ambassador flung himself into the back, lying low. Jim dove into the passenger seat. But before Jim got his door shut, two rebel soldiers grabbed his door. Mac responded instantly, shooting one in the head, two bullets to the chest of the other. Two more were running toward the front of the car. Jim reached down and grabbed the MP5, then opened fire through the open passenger window, dropping the rebels. Mac went to put the Jeep into drive when a rebel soldier that had been hit rolled a hand grenade under the front of the vehicle. The explosion shattered the engine, floorboards under the steering column, and parts of the dash went flying back. Smoke filled the cab. Mac moaned as two chunks of medal were forced through her right thigh. The ambassador had a gash on his head, blood cascading down his face. Jim was bruised but unhurt; he shot the rebel.

"Grab the satellite phone and follow me. Stay low." Mac's leg bled badly, chunks of metal sticking out through the skin. He dragged her along the ground to a cluster of oak trees, maybe two hundred metres. The ambassador followed, crouched low and terrified. Jim began tearing his shirt into strips to tie off Mac's leg above and below the metal pieces. He knew it was too risky to try pulling them out. Jim knew they were all easy prey now; the only way out was a chopper. He dialled the satellite phone. He

was advised that British Royal Navy aircraft carrier was out in the Mediterranean on a training mission just off the coast of Turkey. A Royal Navy Merlin Helicopter nick-named Junglies from the carrier was on its way. The landing zone was four kilometres from their current location. Four kilometres on foot with an injured agent and a fearful ambassador; it might as well have been four hundred. Rebels were closing in.

Mac was tough, but she couldn't walk; she was barely conscious. Her eyes were closing. He lumped her over his shoulder, slung the MP5 machine gun over his other shoulder, grabbed magazines for the Browning, and shoved them into his pockets. "Stay close," he ordered the ambassador.

The first two kilometres through the bush area went without any resistance. Jim figured they were getting close to the clearing; he could hear the chopper. He could also hear the rebels. He knew if there were rebels on the ground, the chopper would come in hot... front Gatling guns blasting. He kept moving, slowly, quietly, listening for movements nearby. He put his finger over his lips as he turned to the ambassador, who was white with shock. He nodded his head. They could hear the twin blades of the chopper coming in nose-down and at full speed. They started to run. The Junglie Merlin chopper came into view. The M60 machine guns mounted on each side door starting spraying bullets, creating a path for Jim and making a clear space to land.

As the chopper touched down, its weapons went silent and two commandos with MP5s jumped off and started firing. It was all or nothing. Jim rallied his strength and clutched Mac as he bolted for the chopper, the ambassador at his side. As Jim approached the chopper, troopers ran over, grabbed Mac, and secured Woodward, getting them all into the chopper as rebel gunfire began. Before Jim's feet were in the chopper, they were airborne.

The medic worked on Mac, who was unconscious. The ambassador was bandaged. Jim was tossed a shirt. As they approached the deck of the aircraft carrier, some British sailors were cheering. That would be the only acknowledgment of the extraction. No medals, no commendations; it was like it never happened.

An air pocket jostled the airplane, bringing Mac back to the present moment, her hand automatically going to her right thigh. *Like it never happened*, she thought again to herself; but it did happen, like so many other military missions no one ever knows about. She closed her eyes and leaned her head back.

Since Turkey, Mac and Jim had stayed in touch and checked in with each other when they could. Mac would pop in to check on his girls when she was in town, help out where she could. Jim had changed since his wife Helen died; he seemed to take on more jobs, leaving his girls with his parents, Grammy and Grandpa Morrison, more and more. His youngest daughter, Hailey, struggled with her mom's death differently than her sister, Abby. She became rebellious while Abby became more studious. The grandparents did their best, but things were slowly unravelling, and the grandparents were at a loss. They needed Jim to be home more, plain and simple. When Mac read the email again, she figured Hailey had just made another move to create problems for everyone. But Mac was in Canada, and Jim was halfway around the world. She'd reach out and see what was happening. It was the least she could do; she wouldn't even be sitting on the Challenger, sipping her soda, if it wasn't for him. She pulled out her phone and started typing a text to Grammy Morrison, saying she'd be landing in twenty minutes and would give her a call to help straighten things out. Then she'd let Jim know it was all a misunderstanding.

TORONTO HARBOUR, ONTARIO, CANADA

The wind was calm, and the water gently bobbed the catamaran. The Wookies had just saved the world on their last mission, and that certainly warranted a celebration; that's what Cole told Trish when she contacted him. Now that he was back, he had called them all together, and they were drinking heartily on the deck of *Windy Girl,* jostling and joking with each other.

Except for the black double hull of the catamaran and muffled exhaust system, *Windy Girl* was far from just a sailing vessel; she was their mission control. Below deck was a fleet of technology: deep dive computer systems, biometrics, social network analysis, radar for earth, sea, and air, as well as a conference table, sleeping berths (for those all-nighters), a number of coffee machines, and a beer fridge. Cole, a.k.a. Boss, had pulled his team of Wookies out of retirement months ago (they were all reluctantly retired from their field, in any case) to help him investigate the murder of a friend; it had proven to be a hornet's nest of intrigue, but they had pulled together as a strong, invincible team.

Retired undercover cop turned Wookie, Bill Thornton a.k.a. Doc (6'2", 260 pounds of force, his hair as wild and red as his beard), turned to Trish Anderson, a.k.a. Falcon, their computer genius and homicide detective. "Still think the Wookies was the wrong name for our band of heroes?"

"Well, I think heroes might be going a bit far, but…"

"Not too far at all," chirped Charlie Foster, a.k.a. Tuna. He was the team's forensic expert. He had finally loosened his tie after a couple of beers; he always wore a suit and tie. "We absolutely are heroes. We have the wounds to prove it. Come on, we just averted an international political disaster."

"Okay, fine. We're heroes," said Anderson. "I still think only you look like a Wookie, Thornton." Bill gave a ceremonial bow and smiled. She smiled back.

"We were fearless warriors," chimed in JT Harrod, a.k.a. 2Tall. He had coordinated all the munitions during their last assignment and was proud of their success. "That's what a Wookie is. Haven't you watched any *Star Wars,* Anderson?"

"Of course I have," she said. "Okay, it's true, we were fearless. Okay, I like the name," she said under her breath.

"What was that?" said Thornton, enjoying the blush on her cheeks. "I couldn't hear you. What did you say?" He leaned in close to her frame, close enough to smell the hint of citrus from the shampoo she had used that morning. She elbowed him in the ribs.

"Fine. Wookies is a good and fitting name for our band of brave-hearts," she said in a monotone. "Satisfied?"

Thornton just sat back, sipped his beer, and smiled.

Everyone laughed.

"Well, we *are* fearless, and we sure were warriors," said Cole. He held up his bottle, and everyone leaned in to clink glasses and bottles together.

NIAGARA FALLS, ONTARIO, CANADA

Hailey, Nina, and Maddie were having the time of their lives. They had agreed to block their parents on their phones until they were on their way home; otherwise, they knew they'd be getting panicked texts all the time. Instead, they went to the Ripley's Believe It or Not museum (twice), screamed their heads off at the Great Canadian Midway, did the Journey Behind the Falls, and flew in the Niagara Sky-Wheel. They ate cotton candy, popcorn, nachos, hotdogs, and anything fast and free. On the third day, they slept until after lunch and decided it was time to get dressed up, hit the club, and try out their fake IDs. They were ready. Peterborough was barely a dot in their rear-view mirror anymore.

"Let's just stay in bed and watch movies until it's time to get ready," said Hailey.

"Great idea, I'm pooped anyway," said Nina.

"Think we should give our parents a call, let them know we're okay?" asked Maddie.

"Sure, if you want a lecture and a buzzkill for tonight," said Hailey. "We'll call them tomorrow before heading home, that'll be fine."

"Yeah, you're right. It will be a buzzkill to call them now," said Nina.

"And get ready for the lecture of the century," said Hailey.

"Yeah, fuck that," said Maddie. "Throw me a bag of those chips, and let's find a good movie."

"Now you're talking," said Hailey.

When the girls left their room after pizza and pop for dinner, their makeup and fashion ensured they looked like the drinking age on their IDs. They kept looking at each other, not quite believing their transformations. Maddie's long blonde hair was pulled out of the top of her head in a high ponytail secured with a wraparound rhinestone accessory. High, sparkling blue heels made her 5'8" frame even leggier, and the short blue thin-strapped dress was accentuated by her blue-tinged makeup. All 5'3" of Nina was in a grey, tight-fitting dress that made her boobs even bigger; instead of high heels, she had opted for black leather boots that almost reached her hemline. Her short black hair was jelled back. But Hailey stole the show with her thin, lacy black crop-top showing her belly button ring, smocked lacy black mini-skirt that barely covered her ass, black stilettos, Ferrari-red lipstick, and fake eyelashes. Her shoulder-length hair was curled and wavy. She knew her dad and grandparents would die if they saw her dressed like this. They had all painted their nails the same sparkly mauve and wore the same long, dangly earrings and multicoloured bangles. They were ready to hit the town. They all felt like they were in a movie, like *Best Night Ever* that they'd watched repeatedly at sleepovers since they were 13.

They stood on the curb, keenly aware of their hemlines, and waited for a cab, giggling. When the cab pulled to the curb, they curled into the back seat together, and Hailey gave the name of the nightclub they had googled weeks earlier. They whispered and giggled, adjusted hair and jewelry, admired each other's outfits, checked for their lipstick in their sequinned small clutch bags, and then stepped out in front of the nightclub. The huge entrance with the even bigger lights took them by surprise. They calmly walked to the back of the line, which wasn't too long, and waited to get to the door, nervous about their IDs. They watched and listened. A fight broke out as they approached the door.

Nina leaned in to Maddie. "Maybe this isn't such a good idea."

Maddie elbowed her in the ribs as the security guard approached them. He asked for IDs. They pulled out their cards just as he was pushed from behind, and they were waved through.

A young man leaning against the hood of his sports car watched them walk inside, a little wobbly on their oversized heels. He smiled thinly, took a drag on his cigarette, and flicked it into the street. He smoothed his hair, tucked the tails of his metallic blue collared shirt inside his designer jeans, and strode into the Dragonfly.

The music was so loud the girls couldn't hear their

own thoughts, let alone others'. There were people everywhere.

Sitting.

Standing.

Drinking.

Dancing.

Laughing.

Kissing.

Fondling.

The trio made their way over to the bar, a long slab of white marble, standing room only. Bottles of different sizes and shapes filled with alcohol from around the world were illuminated by multicoloured lights glowing from behind; the rest of the wall behind the bar looked like a piece of art by Mondrian with digital projections of statues and moving colours inside black frames. The girls felt their senses overload. They ordered the drinks they'd rehearsed: two strawberry daiquiris and a margarita. It was to be their first experience with alcohol. With no cover charge that night, the cost of drinks was exorbitant. Their cash would be gone faster than they had anticipated. Luckily, Maddie had stolen her mom's credit card. They had thought of everything.

The alcohol exploded into their veins on the first sip, spiking every nerve and muscle and brain cell. They swooned and savoured the next mouthful, revelling in the buzz. After a few more gulps to empty their glasses (they had yet to learn the art of sipping), they plopped them onto the bar. The bartender moved in their direction.

"Three more," announced Maddie, waving to him, feeling like she was in a movie. Then she pulled her friends onto the dance floor. They moved as a trio, wide-eyed and curious about everyone around them.

"Happy birthday, BFF," Nina and Maddie screeched into Hailey's ear. They all laughed and tossed their hair, shook their bangles, and moved their bodies to song after song. Hailey wiped the perspiration off her brow.

"Time for those drinks." And she started back to the bar, lifted her glass, and bottomed it. Her friends drank half.

"Another round," called Hailey.

"And some water, please," said Nina, puffing her dress in and out for air. "God, it's hot in here."

Hailey lifted her next drink into the air, spilling some onto her dress as she made a toast. "To my besties."

The other two did the same, and they clinked glasses then bottomed them.

"Let's do shots next," said Nina.

"Oh yeah, remember that TikTok video where they had those shots lined up and just downed one at a time?" said Maddie.

"Right, and then turned the shot glass upside down on the counter. Yeah, let's do that."

"Bartender, shots please," said Hailey.

"Of what?" asked the bartender.

The girls looked at each other, wide-eyed. "Surprise us," said Maddie.

The bartender brought over three shot glasses and poured amber-coloured whiskey into each one. "Whiskey," he said and walked away.

The girls each picked up a shot, looked at each other, giggled, and pounded them back before turning over the shot glass, and banging it onto the bar. Hailey waved at the bartender.

"Three more," she said. Nina and Maddie leaned forward, almost falling off their chairs, and laughed, shaking Hailey's shoulders.

"Man, I want a birthday like this when I turn 16," said Maddie.

"Me too," Nina chimed in.

They laughed and tumbled off their chairs, tripping on the way back to the dance floor, laughing again. It was crowded. People were bumping into each other and hands were roaming. Maddie felt a hand on her ass and turned around to the smile of a very tall man. She grinned and grabbed Nina's hand. They kept dancing, getting into the flow of the crowd. Nina turned to look for the man, secretly hoping he would come back. She was feeling tingly and free. She wanted his hand on her ass again.

They were all high on alcohol, pulsing lights, throbbing music, body heat, and adrenaline.

A man in a metallic blue shirt moved up against Hailey, pressing his crotch against her hip. She had the vibe he wanted. Nina felt him move closer as they were all standing so close together. She winked at Hailey, wondering if there was someone who would come over to her. Maddie was looking for that guy. Hailey turned, and her face was inches from the face wearing the blue metallic shirt. He smiled and kissed her. She kissed him back, her head swimming. He pulled her away from the other girls.

"Another drink, sexy?" he yelled into her ear. She just smiled and pointed to the bar. He pulled her over to where the shots of whiskey sat, handed her one, and held the other up in a toast. He tossed his back. She did the same. He cracked the shot glass upside down on the bar, took hers, and did the same, then he pulled her in for a long, deep kiss, his hand roaming around her backside. The other girls goggled at them.

He pulled her back onto the floor and started to dirty-dance with her. Hailey was lost in him.

"Come for a drive with me, let's get out of here," he yelled loudly into her ear, grabbing her lobe with his teeth and then moving his tongue around the edge of her ear. Hailey felt a heat pass through her groin and down her legs. She moved closer to him. She nodded and turned to the girls.

"I'm going for a drive with him," she yelled.

"Hailey, no, we agreed we would stay together." But their voices were lost in the alcohol, loud music, and sweaty, pulsing bodies.

Hailey smiled as he grabbed her hand, pulling her toward the door. When her friends tried to follow, they were swallowed by the crowd, and Maddie felt the same hand on her ass. She turned, smiling, and started to dance.

EASTERN RIDGE GOLF AND COUNTRY CLUB, KINGSTON, ONTARIO, CANADA

Andrej Sokol leaned back in his leather chair, swivelling around to look at the rolling greens, fairways, and bunkers of the golf course behind him. It was a busy day with golfers addressing their balls in the T-box, carts racing across fairways to find their shot, and players leaning on clubs waiting while a putt was being sized up. He loved to sit and watch the peace unfolding outside his office window.

It was an office as neat as a pin. His designer desk was a showpiece of smoky tempered glass sitting atop a pedestal of four reinforced golf clubs. There were just a few items on the surface: a seventeen-inch laptop, a coffee mug with his Eastern Ridge Golf and Country Club logo, and a silver phone complete with numbers to push and a handle connected with a curly cord to the base. No pens. No paper. He had a secretary for that kind of thing. Beyond the desk sat two dark green wing-backed chairs with a three-sided black onyx table between them. The walls were covered with photographs of Sokol and legends of the game shaking hands: Jack Nicklaus, Tiger Woods, Arnold Palmer, Mike Wire, Dustin Johnson, Adam Hadwin, and an attractive young female player hoisting her winning trophy for all to see. She was about 25 years of age, with long, lean, shapely legs, well displayed in every golf outfit she wore. Her perfect white teeth gleamed inside her smile while her braided brown hair was pulled over her left shoulder, hanging down past her breasts, which were well presented in her golf blouse. Her name was Miranda Sokol.

The knock on the door caused Andrej to swivel his chair back to his face his desk and the door. "Enter," he commanded.

The door opened a crack, and two green eyes peeked around the corner.

"Okay to come in, Dad?"

"Of course, of course," he said, his tone softening just slightly. Andrej got up and walked across the room to greet his daughter. He hugged her, kissed her cheek, and led her over to the chairs. They both sat down. She crossed her ankles, her pink golf skirt barely covering the top of her thighs, the sleeveless white-pink-polka-dot-moisture-wicking shirt clinging to her perspiration-covered back. She'd just finished eighteen holes.

"Good round?" asked her dad.

"Better. Not where I want to be, but better."

"You'll get there. You'll crack the top ten on the LPGA tour this year." He paused, looking Miranda up and down. "Have you considered wearing long pants on course? I don't like your outfit choices."

"Why? What's wrong with them." She looked down at her pink skirt, one of her favourites.

"Makes you look a bit too easy."

"What? No. Pants are too restrictive. Plus everyone wears these outfits now. Actually, all the sponsors encourage it. You know that, Dad."

"Doesn't mean I agree with it. You don't need to be selling yourself out there."

Miranda rolled her eyes. "Okay, Dad, fine. I'll consider it, but right now, I want to win our mixed tournament. You still have me paired with Cole Buckman, right?"

"I do. But he hasn't confirmed yet. I have you down with Jordan Speith if Buckman can't make it." Miranda pursed her lips. "I know you prefer Buckman, but I can't drag him here in chains." He laughed at his own joke.

"It's a big tournament, Dad. Not many courses do a mixed golf experience like this. And a player's world rankings are affected by a win. I want the best to team up with me. Plus Cole does know the course; he's played here a lot of times. I'm sure he'll come. Call his agent again."

"Is that the only reason you want Buckman?" He lifted an eyebrow.

Miranda put on her little girl pouty face and smiled at her dad. "Of course it is." She looked up to the ceiling attempting to keep a straight face.

"I'll let you know by the end of the week."

"Will you call his agent again?"

He clearly wasn't pleased with her insistence. "Miranda, I will get to it."

"The tournament…"

"Miranda, ENOUGH."

She considered the pout again but changed her mind and the subject. Seeing that all too familiar look on his face and hearing that tone in his voice, she backed off quickly. She had felt the back of his hand more than once growing up… and watched her mother get worse. She knew when to stop. "Think Mom will be back in time for the tournament?"

"She's here now."

"No, she's not. She was just given the post of minister of justice. She's pretty busy and has a lot more responsibility."

"Yes, of course, I know." His face remained unchanged as his mind whirled around his fabrication, and he didn't miss a beat with his immediate reply. "I'll see what her schedule is."

"It's okay, Dad, I'll let her know. She has to take a break at some point."

"We both know she isn't very good at that." He stood up, leaned over, and gave her a kiss on the forehead, his face stoic. "It will all be fine." He gave her knee a little pat and went back to his desk. Miranda knew the conversation was over. She hesitated only a moment and then let herself out, closing the large oak door behind her, pausing for a moment to inhale a long breath, something she always needed after an interaction with her dad.

Andrej went back to sit at his desk and waited until the door clicked into place behind Miranda. He picked up his phone.

NIAGARA FALLS, ONTARIO, CANADA

The room smelled of stale cigarettes and feet. Faded blotches scattered across the once rust-coloured carpet bled into the nicotine-stained once cream-coloured walls. There was a crack in the window adjacent to the door. Blinds with missing and ripped vanes hung at an angle across the panes. A tube TV stood on a chipped dresser, handles missing on some drawers.

A small girl cowered by the door.

Her smooth white skin was drained of colour by fear, green eyes dilated like a mouse in a trap, a fake eyelash hanging awkwardly by the corner of her eye, the mascara mingling with tears, creating stains around her eyes and into her overly blushed cheeks. Her Ferrari-red lipstick was smeared along her right cheek. She kept trying to pull down her short black skirt with her free arm, wishing she had a jacket to cover the cropped black top she was wearing, revealing her navel piercing. Strands of her shoulder-length hair, so curled and coifed by Maddie and Nina just hours earlier, was now limp and kept falling into her face.

A man of around five-ten with a heavy build, thick arms, hair on his knuckles, greasy short hair, wearing jeans and a green and orange Hawaiian shirt, closed the door to the room. He leaned his back against the door, adjusting the Glock in the back of his belt. The other man, about six-foot-two, was thin but muscular. Thick gold chains hung around his neck, gold bracelets around his wrists, and ringlets of yellow hair down to his shoulders. He wore Balenciaga limited-edition streetwear with designer white shoes. His thumb and forefinger touched as it wrapped around the forearm of the young girl. He dragged her farther into the room, standing with her in front of the sagging double bed, the faded blue comforter pulled tight across its frame, pillows cowering underneath. The third man leaned on the peeling lime green paint of the door frame leading to the bathroom, facing the foot of the bed. He had short-cropped hair jelled up in the centre of his head. He had squashed his bulky five-foot-six frame into a Gucci suit. He wore rings on every finger. His eyes took in every curve of his new recruit. A speck of drool appeared on his lower lip. He licked it away, eager to put her to work. His boss would be pleased with this one. He'd like to give her a test drive later himself, but Shadow Man would be pissed. He may already be pissed that he'd expanded their working turf on his own without his approval. At that moment, Leonard felt it would be worth the risk.

Those six pairs of eyes stared at her through the masks they all wore: skin-toned plastic with five holes for breath around the mouth, a nose outdent, and hollow eye sockets. Their voices sounded muffled from behind the goalie masks, which was the point.

"I'm going out to get some food and water. It's after midnight. We have to get her cleaned up at least. She'll have her first customer soon. We'll have to set things up. Then find a new location. Remember, one of us has to be outside the door at all times in case we got a runner. Got it?" The other two nodded. "You take sentry duty tonight." Leonard poked the Hawaiian shirt and walked out the door. The girl jumped as it banged shut.

"Maybe she needs a test drive, know what I mean?"

"Leonard said no test drive, but maybe a little sample, get her warmed up."

The guy holding her arm reached his other hand around and slowly slid it up the inside of her leg, moved her panties to one side, and ran his finger around her pussy. She winced, recoiled, and tried to push him away. He smiled at her as he stood back and licked his finger, then pushed her onto the bed. He turned to the Hawaiian shirt. "Fuck, I hope he brings back two large pizzas. I'm starving."

The girl pulled herself up and sat on the edge of the bed, leaned over, and puked on the floor.

The Hawaiian shirt looked down at the puke, pulling his collar over his nose. "Clean it up."

"How?"

Hawaiian shirt stared and moved to the door, opening it and stepping out. "LEONARD," he hollered. Leonard turned around. "You didn't needle her."

The girl ran to the window. She was looking onto a parking lot. She ran back and scanned the place for another window. Nothing. The doorknob rattled. She dove under the bed.

"Where the fuck is she?"

"Well, she has to be here."

She watched their feet move around the room, wondering if she could make it to the door in time. But before she could make move, her feet were grabbed. She clung to the frame of the bed, slicing her finger open on a protruding nail as they pulled. She screamed and kicked, but they pulled her out and flung her onto the bed.

Leonard moved forward. "Fuck. Should have done this when we brought her in. Hold her down." It was easy for tanks to restrain a toothpick. Leonard secured the tourniquet onto her forearm. She couldn't squirm or scream, but her eyes rolled white and wide. He sucked the heroin into the syringe and unloaded it into her vein. Her eyes closed. The tourniquet went back into his pocket with the syringe.

"Can we take these motherfuckin' masks off now?"

Leonard nodded, and they tossed them into the chair by the window.

"Now I'm going for the fucking pizza." Leonard left the room and hopped into his car.

TORONTO HARBOUR, ONTARIO, CANADA

The *Windy Girl* gently rocked in her slip, lulling Bill into a comforting nap below deck… until his phone started buzzing.

"Yeah," he answered groggily.

"Rise and shine, sweetheart, we will all be over there in a few minutes," said Cole.

"Thanks for the warning."

"Hey, I did call."

The line went dead, and Bill pulled himself into a sitting position. Everyone else had places to rest their head and keep their clothes, but *Windy Girl* was Bill's home these days. He realized he better pick up the clothes all over the floor and do a quick sweep for dirty dishes. As he washed the last dish and tossed the last pair of sock in the hamper, he heard voices on deck and climbed up.

"Well, if it isn't the Wookies."

They all hugged and stood, waiting for Cole.

"Let's go below deck for this," Cole said. Charlie, Trish, 2Tall, and Bill eyed each other. Something was definitely up. Bill had put on a pot of coffee, and everyone poured themselves a mug and sat down.

"What's up, Cole?" 2Tall said.

"It's just a text, so I don't have the whole picture yet. That's where you guys come in."

"Who's it from?" asked Trish.

"Mac," said Cole.

"Oooooo," they all teased in unison.

"It's not like that, unfortunately." He smiled.

They drank slowly.

No one spoke.

"Remember Mac talking about Jim Morrison?" They all nodded. "Well, his daughter Hailey is apparently missing, and her two friends. Have been for a few days. Mac thought it was just girl stuff, but she seems worried. And if she's worried…"

"We're worried," said Bill.

"Yeah. Mac doesn't worry easily, so I'm thinking we need to look into this," Cole said.

"How old is she?" asked Trish.

"Sixteen. Sixteen three days ago."

"A birthday blitz," said Trish.

"How long have they been missing?" asked Bill.

"Three days. Long enough for the parents to be concerned…" Cole started.

"…and not long enough for the police to take it seriously," 2Tall finished.

"Exactly."

They all paused, soaking in the potential gravity of the situation.

"So Mac wants us to find her and the other girls," said Bill.

"Yeah. Police aren't doing much."

"Not much they can do," Charlie put in.

"Do we know anything else at all?" asked Trish.

"Not at this point," said Cole. "But the mom of one of the girls, Maddie, I think, gave her younger son the third degree, and he cracked and told her they had gone to Niagara Falls."

"Girls love to talk," said Trish. "And they haven't called home, I'm guessing."

"No."

"So they've turned their phones off, which is highly unlikely; they've blocked their parents to not get a lecture, but they're still using their phones. They are doing something illegal."

"Like what?" Charlie asked.

"They are 16. They probably have fake IDs," said Trish. "Problem is, they're girls."

"Meaning…?" said Bill.

"Meaning if they were boys on a tear, that would be one thing, but girls on a tear are at risk."

"At risk of being picked up," said Bill.

"And not for ice cream," said Charlie.

"There are a lot of crime organizations in Niagara Falls," Trish said.

"Fuck, yes," said Bill.

"Not good," said 2Tall.

"Not good at all," added Charlie.

"Well, if there is a chance that what Trish is saying is true, and there is a very high chance of that, we have to work fast here," Cole said.

"Agreed," they all said in unison.

"We have to get her before she disappears, assuming the worst," Bill said.

"Okay, I'm going to do some masquerading on the dark web, do some fishing and some planting," said Trish.

"Trish, what kind of planting exactly?" asked 2Tall.

"One that will get the crime rings talking, worrying, wondering if someone is infringing on turf. That kind. The best way to get the attention of these pricks is to go for the ego." She looked around the group.

"She's right," said Charlie, almost to himself. His shoulders had hunched up.

"Of course I'm right," said Trish. "Hey, you okay, Charlie?"

"Yeah, yeah. I'm good. This kind of crime ring makes my blood run cold."

"Ice-cold," added Bill. "So Trish, you're going down a human trafficking hole, organized crime hangout, correct?"

"Correct."

"Okay, while she's doing that, we need more info on the girl," added 2Tall.

"Right. I'm going to call Mac and have a longer

discussion. Let her know we're moving on it and find out what I can," said Cole.

Trish felt herself sweating through her blouse as she sat down at the computer. If the worst had happened and a crime group had grabbed the girls, they had a ridiculously small window to find them before she went missing.

NIAGARA FALLS, ONTARIO, CANADA

Maddie and Nina sat on the end of the bed in their hotel room.

After Hailey left, Maddie had started dancing with the guy who had his hand on her ass. Soon his hand was on her breast, and one was up her skirt. She had pulled herself away, desperately searching for Nina. She saw her kissing a guy at the bar. She went over, tossed back another shot, and started pulling on Nina's shoulder.

"I'm a little busy here," yelled Nina.

"Where's Hailey?"

"Isn't she back?"

"No, she's not." Maddie was starting to sway. She had to keep blinking her eyes to see clearly.

"Fuck, how long has she been gone?"

"A lot of shots ago, I don't fucking know."

"Think she went back to the hotel?"

"I can't hear you. We need to get out of here."

They agreed to go back to the hotel and hailed a cab. They were having trouble walking. When they got to their hotel room, they had to pour the contents of their handbags onto the floor to find the room card. And then it took a while to get the door open.

"Hurry up, I'm gonna puke," said Maddie, bolting into the bathroom when the door opened.

Nina was sitting on the end of the bed when she came out. "She's not here."

"It's past midnight. Try her cell." No response.

"Should we call the police?"

"And say what, that we were illegally drinking in a place we shouldn't have been in?"

"Right. Call home?"

Maddie just stared at her.

"What if she gave someone our hotel room number and they'll be coming here?"

"What if she's in trouble?"

"What do we do?"

Suddenly, the movie *Best Night Ever* had turned into the movie *Eight Days*. Eight days… they couldn't wait eight more seconds.

They didn't know what to do.

TORONTO HARBOUR, ONTARIO, CANADA

"I got a bite!" Trish hollered, arms in the air. She'd been monitoring her screens for hours.

It was 1:30 a.m. Trish's voice woke up Charlie and 2Tall, who had dozed off on the cabin cots. Bill and Cole shimmied down to the cabin from the cockpit. Trish waited until everyone was seated around the table.

"I got a bite."

"How exactly?" 2Tall asked.

"Is this really the time for a lengthy explanation?" Trish said.

"Well…"

"Do I ask you if your guns are loaded or if you've chosen the right weapons? I mean this is…"

"Okay, I see where this is going. Just give us the skinny on your process, Trish," Cole said.

"Fine. I did some onion routing. Then I used anonymizing browsers like Tor and Ahmia, usually a few different ones. Then…"

"What do those browsers do?" 2Tall asked.

"Simply, it means hundreds of criminals around the world redirect my nodes through a series of proxy servers so it stays 'off the grid.' And that's all done through our VPN to further encrypt my conversations."

"And that's all legal?" Charlie asked.

"Well, the conversation is legal. Who I'm conversing with is illegal." She turned and looked at 2Tall. "That help?" she asked with a sarcastic look.

2Tall was stone-faced. "I think I'll stick to my weapons," he said sheepishly.

"Good," said Trish. "Can I finish what I started to say about the bite?"

"YES," they all said in unison.

"Okay… those crime ring fuckers hate it when someone encroaches on their turf. They are very territorial. That's how organized crime wars begin. Anyway, I don't have to explain it all, and it doesn't matter anyway. Here's the Coles notes." They all smiled and looked at Cole.

Cole smiled. "Works on all levels."

Trish continued. "I said that someone new was trafficking girls on the turf in Niagara. It caught heat. It spread fast. I cozied up to the pissed-off group, the established crime ring in that area. Told them I liked dealing with them and didn't want someone new bringing in girls. That created a huge pile of manure. They wanted these new 'Romeos' taught a lesson…" She took a breath and surveyed the room. "The name of two motels popped up, sort of like holding cells until the girls get moved. Innkeepers take money under the table to provide this service."

"Nice of them," sneered 2Tall.

"How long do we have?" Cole asked.

"I'd say tomorrow. Maybe six, seven in the morning. Maybe."

"That means we have until 4:00 a.m. Do we have an address?" Cole asked.

Trish handed him a paper. "I don't know which one to try first."

"Could there be more than these two?" Thornton aside.

"Yup."

"I'll get the weapons," 2Tall said.

"I'll take my truck, scope out other possible locations," Bill offered.

"2Tall and I will go to the two on Trish's list," Cole said.

"I'll stay back to man the phones," Charlie said.

"Good, because if things heat up, I can't monitor screens and phones," Trish put in.

"Charlie, call Mac, tell her to run some interference, make sure the police stay off our tail. We will be racing all the way to Niagara."

"On it."

"Let's roll," 2Tall said.

Trish gestured at them. "Wait, one more thing. In those web conversations, a couple of eight-balls of harry was purchased yesterday in Niagara."

"Fuck, they've pumped them with heroin already." Bill turned and left the group, digging in a back cupboard.

"Pray those girls don't nod out before you get there. They won't be careful how much they loaded into that syringe at all," Charlie said.

"Cole." He turned as Bill sent a small container sailing toward him. Cole caught it and looked at him, head tilted to one side in question. "It's a naloxone kit. One for your ride, one for mine. Just in case they've been injected. May save their lives."

"Cole," called Trish. He turned around, and she tossed him a key fob. "Take my Jeep. It has a full tank of gas."

"We've gotta move."

NIAGARA FALLS, ONTARIO, CANADA

Hailey's eyes fluttered open. It was 1:00 a.m. Her mouth was dry as toast. She couldn't feel her tongue. The room seemed to be heaving. Then all she could smell was pizza, like there was pizza everywhere; she couldn't stop smelling it. The room was filled with pizza. She didn't know where she was; her head was pounding. She pulled herself up and swayed from side to side. That pizza smell again. There was a piece in a box beside her. She reached over with what felt like an oversized hand and grabbed the slice, shoving it into her mouth, craving the smell, the taste. She swallowed. A bottle of water appeared in front of her, and she snatched it before it could disappear, gulping the liquid, feeling it float through her body. She looked up. And everything started spinning. The Hawaiian shirt filled her field of vision. She threw up the pizza and shrivelled back onto the bed, unconscious.

"Oh, Jesus. I'm not cleaning puke again."

Leonard's phone rang. "It's Him. Watch her." He went outside, lit a cigarette, and answered the phone.

"Hey man, I have some good news. I've cracked into a new—"

"What the fuck. What the fuck are you doing?"

"It's all—"

"SHUT THE FUCK UP, LEONARD. You have stirred

serious shit, that's what you have done. Turf is turf, and you're on someone else's. Why the fuck did I not know about this? FUCK. Misha is on his way with the van. He'll be there around three thirty. Put the little bitch in the van and get the fuck out of there."

"What about the guys I hired?"

"From where?"

"From our turf, our zone."

"Fine, bring them too. We were down a girl anyway. From now on, everything goes through me. Every fucking thing. Got it?"

"Got it."

"Just sit tight until Misha gets there. Don't do any thinking. Don't DO anything. Just sit there and wait. Hear me?"

"Yes, I fucking hear you. But what about the other girls? I have a few more lined up."

"That's Hajek's turf, you moron. Get the fuck out of there."

PETERBOROUGH, ONTARIO, CANADA

It was well after midnight. Grammy Morrison brought another pot of coffee to the table. Her husband poured. Maddie and Nina's parents sat around the table with them. None of the girls were answering their phones or replying to texts. The waiting was intolerable.

"We have extra rooms upstairs if anyone is tired," Mrs. Morrison offered.

"There is no way I can sleep," said Nina's mother. Everyone nodded in agreement.

"I just hope we hear from the girls soon," said Maddie's dad. "I'm not sure how long I can take this." His wife placed her hand on top of his.

They all sipped in silence.

Two cell phones on the table started to ring and buzz at the same time. Maddie and Nina's parents dove forward, clicking the answer icon.

"Hello, hello," voices appealed in unison.

"Put it on speaker, Gloria."

Gloria clicked the icon. Static filled the room.

There was a long pause. Everyone held their breath. Then, sobbing, crying.

Nina's mom spoke first. "Nina? Honey? Is that you?"

"Mom."

Nina's mom clamped her hand over her mouth to stifle

a cry, and her husband put his arm around her. "Mom, I'm sorry, I'm so sorry."

"Honey, no sorrys. Are you okay?"

"Yeah."

"And Maddie?"

The other phone came to life. "Mom?" Maddie's mom started to cry. Her dad sat with his head in his hands.

"Where is Hailey?" called out Grandpa Morrison.

There was a deadening silence, like the one that hovers between bursts of thunder, and then, one of the girls whispered, "We don't know."

Everyone in the room stopped breathing. Grammy Morrison left the table and the room.

Maddie's father broke the silence. "What do you mean you don't know?"

"She left with this guy, and she didn't come back." The girls couldn't stop crying.

"Wait a minute," interjected Nina's mom. "What guy? Where are you?"

"We were at a night club in Niagara Falls," said Nina.

"WHAT THE FUCK?!" said the dads simultaneously. Anger had replaced fear.

"Dad, we fucked up. We're scared. What do we do?" Maddie started to weep, her breath coming in gasps.

"Where are you now?" her dad asked.

"Nina and I are back at the motel," said Nina.

"It might not be safe there anymore," he told her.

Grandpa Morrison wiped his eyes and put his head into his hands. The parents all looked to one another in shock. They had no clue what to do. They felt almost catatonic with a mix of anger and fear.

Grammy Morrison stood quietly in the kitchen, listening, leaning on the counter, finding her rational thoughts. Then she reached up into the cupboard and grabbed the bottle of Glenfiddich. She stood cradling the bottle in her hands, remembering how she had pulled it out the night her daughter-in-law Helen died. She had been walking on the sidewalk when a car bounced over the curb and smashed into her, then a telephone pole. Drunk driver. At first they thought Helen might pull through in the hospital, but there had been too much internal damage.

Hailey had been 10 years old, Abby 14. Devastating. Jim had been overseas. Grief seemed to be a constant and uninvited guest in the Morrison household after that. Jim started to take more assignments; Abby buried herself in her high school classes; Hailey buried herself in her room. Mrs. Morrison, a retired high school teacher, knew that sharp kids going down the wrong path was a dangerous recipe. She dearly hoped that wasn't going to be Hailey, but the writing was starting to appear on the wall. She was becoming more and more withdrawn. Moving from the base in Petawawa to Peterborough had made sense at the time: less isolation, grandparents close by, better schools, more for the girls to do. But the bigger town brought problems as well… more to do didn't always lead to Girl Guides or the soccer team.

Mrs. Morrison poured herself a shot of the scotch and downed it. She took a deep breath. Someone had to take charge. It was time to make some decisions. She pulled her phone out of her pocket and started texting. She had a plan for Maddie and Nina. She put her faith in Mac to get Hailey back. It was the only immediate option. She slid the phone back into her pocket, picked up the bottle, and went back into the room filled with conflicting emotions. She immediately started to pour the scotch into each coffee mug. Then she placed the bottle on the table and put her hand up, asking for silence.

"Maddie, Nina, this is Grammy Morrison. You girls need to get out of there now. Go down to the front office in the hotel and tell them to call you a taxi. Not an Uber, a taxi. Don't do it yourself. Have someone at the front desk do it, and stand there while you wait. We are going to send you a photo of a credit card. Give it to the driver. Tell him to take you to this address in Hamilton. We will text that too. It is my niece. Stay there with them. They will keep you safe until your mom and dad show up to get you."

She sat down and took a mouthful of her drink. Nina's dad didn't question a thing. He pulled out his credit card, took a photo, and sent it to his daughter. Grammy Morrison scribbled the name and address of her niece on a piece of paper, and he sent that in a text.

"Girls," said Maddie's mom, "did you hear all that?"

"Yes."

"Are you going?"

"We're already out the door," said Maddie.

"What about Hailey?" asked Nina.

"We'll find her," said Grandpa Morrison. "Goddamnit, we will find her," he whispered to himself.

"Text us when you are in the taxi," said Nina's dad.

"Okay."

"Nina, Maddie?" said Grammy Morrison.

"Yeah?"

"Get into that taxi as fast as you can."

"And stay by the front desk until you see the taxi," interjected Nina's dad.

"We love you," they all said in unison.

The call disconnected.

TORONTO HARBOUR, ONTARIO, CANADA

"Want a coffee, Trish?" asked Charlie.

"That would be amazing. Thanks. I just don't want to leave the screens for a minute. Things change constantly, and I can't miss a move."

"Yeah, totally get it." He poured the coffee, added a bit of sugar that he thought she could probably use, and put the mug down beside her.

She lifted it to her lips, sipped, and took a deep breath. "Perfect. Thanks, Charlie."

"Of course… Hey, Trish, look at this." Charlie was pointing to a text on his phone.

"Yeah, we're getting all of Cole's texts now. He usually redirects them to us when he's in the field. Looks like the other girls are safe. So it's just Hailey that's missing now."

"Should we let the team know?" asked Charlie.

"Yeah, give Bill a call."

Charlie dialled Bill's number. He told Bill to relay the info to Cole and 2Tall.

"Hey, Charlie, if you don't mind me asking, what happened earlier? I've never seen you pale and tense up like that before. I mean, you're the guy that keeps fingers in jars in your basement. I've never seen you flinch. What happened?"

"A memory. One that still haunts me."

"Care to share? I won't even look at you because I have to stay glued to these screens, so you could just talk, you know, if you want to. Things are a bit quiet right now, so talk if you want to." She kept sipping at her coffee, staring at the screens while she spoke.

Charlie took a long breath. He felt it was time to tell the story. Share the burden. He'd held it close for a long time.

"It was more than forty years ago, in Gananoque. I was in love with this girl, Cynthia. She was about 16, I was around 20. She wanted to be a doctor. Worked so hard. Was just brilliant and beautiful. Deep brown eyes, bouncy brown hair. We often joked that our careers would be a good fit… forensic scientist, medical doctor. And we had it all planned out: when our wedding would be, how many kids, how we'd juggle it all. We just had such a great connection." He paused and smiled at the recollection, lifting his coffee mug to his lips. "She was saving up for school and worked a number of different jobs. This one night she was working a late shift at the dry cleaners, and I was going to pick her up after work, take her for pizza. I decided to arrive a bit early and help her close up. As I rounded the corner I heard screams. I started to run, and then I saw it… three guys were dragging Cynthia down the street. I went into overdrive, racing toward her. I saw her fighting them off, how she fell and hit her head on the sidewalk, how they pulled her up and punched her on the side of the head. I couldn't get my legs to move fast enough. I could hardly breathe. But I was closing in, and they hadn't seen me. They were dragging her toward a van parked at the curb. I wanted to tear them limb from limb. Just as they slid the side door open, I leapt forward, landing on the guy holding her. I remember the blood streaming down her face. I pushed her free and landed a punch full-force into the guy's face, knocking him into the van. The other two came at me, but I was in attack mode. I slid the door onto the one guy's hand, crushing it, taking off his finger. He was screaming and writhing in pain. The other guy ran. I bent down and picked up the finger: it was my first."

Charlie was breathless. The boat was quiet except for the occasional beep from the computer screens and water lapping against the hulls.

"Jesus, Charlie, I had no idea." Trish swivelled in her chair and faced him. "Did you get a look at them?"

"No, they were wearing balaclavas. I wanted to kill those motherfuckers."

Trish took a breath and pursed her lips. "Did you run the prints off the one finger you got?"

"Yup, nothing came up. Guess they never got caught. Fuckers. But it's still in a jar in my basement."

"What happened to Cynthia?"

"That punch to the head left her permanently blind."

"Holy fuck."

"Yeah, and she pulled away from everyone, including me. Stopped doing everything—work, school."

"Were they a trafficking gang?"

"I don't know. I've been trying to find that bastard for years. But he's a ghost."

"Where is Cynthia now?"

"She eventually went back to school, but not for a medical degree. She works as a counsellor with the blind now."

"That's pretty awesome."

"Yeah, it really is. Amazing woman."

"Do you still see her?"

"I keep in touch. Helped pay for her school. Always take her out for her birthday. We do talk."

"Did she ever marry?"

"Nope. Lives with her sister."

"You still love her, don't you?"

Charlie got really quiet. "I do. But for a long time I think seeing me reminded her of that night, which kind of ended our romance. It changed both our lives. I just married my work I guess."

Trish turned back to the computer screens. A wind had come up and was gently swaying *Windy Girl* side to side.

"You know, Tom Downs worked homicide back then. If those thugs ever killed anyone, he would've found them."

"Tom Downs, yeah, I remember him. Good guy. Great at his job. You're right, he would've tracked them down for sure. How do you know him?"

"When I was promoted to the homicide division, I was paired with Tom Downs as my senior partner."

Charlie did a long, slow whistle. "Didn't you fall into the pot of gold at the end of the rainbow. He was a fucking legend in homicide. Still is."

"Yeah, I know. To this day I still don't know how that happened, but what a partner to start with. He was amazing. Taught me everything I know."

"So that's why you're so good." Charlie winked and punched her in the arm. "He hated leaving a case unsolved, but he did have a few cold cases. I remember one that really stuck in his craw was, geez, what was it he called that case, something like a colour… ummm.."

"Yeah, I remember. The Yellow Briar Farm case."

"Right. That's it. Did he ever talk about it?"

"No. Would just clam right up. And Tom liked to talk."

"That he did. Odd about that case. He kept those facts pretty close."

"That happened before I started working with him too."

"You stay in touch?"

"Oh yeah. We chat here and there. I will sometimes run stuff by him and we will play a round of golf once in a while."

"Is he retired?"

"Are any of us retired?"

"Good point." They high-fived. "Want a refill?" asked Charlie.

"More than sex and chocolate!" They both laughed, and Charlie took her mug, pouring more dark liquid inside, and a bigger spoon of sugar.

"Charlie?"

"Yeah."

"Has she softened toward you over the years? Like, do you have a chance with her now?"

"I don't know."

"Do you want to know?"

Charlie concentrated on pouring more coffee into his mug. Then he turned and looked right at Trish. "Yes. There's never been anyone else. Yes, I really do."

NIAGARA FALLS, ONTARIO, CANADA

Cole and 2Tall were racing down the QEW highway west at about 160 km/hr in Anderson's grey Grand Cherokee. Doc was close behind in his black F-150. At that hour of the morning, the usually bumper-to-bumper highway was all but deserted. As they approached the city limits of Niagara Falls, 2Tall punched the address of the first motel into the GPS. Fifteen minutes, said the device. They watched Doc fork off the highway toward a cluster of motels; they had coordinated en route with the help of Falcon and Tuna.

As they drove down the streets, houses were still shrouded in sleepy darkness. Only a few had the blue glow of a flat-screen television shining through the window of shift workers or night owls; or predators.

Cole was in combat mode, wary and sharp.

He spun around the last corner indicated by the GPS Falcon had programmed and slowed down. A motel sign glared ahead in seventies neon yellow, the letters arranged in a vertical line. Light bulbs circled around the word *Motel,* flashing off and on, many burned out or broken. The *No* in the red *Vacancy* sign by the office was turned on; the parking lot was virtually deserted. Cole coasted in quietly, the crunch of gravel under his tires the only sound. He stopped the car. It idled patiently as they exited, leaving the doors ajar. Cole attached the silencer to the threaded barrel of his Glock 19 and allowed it to wait at the end of his arm, slightly behind his back, just out of sight… the beauty of such a compact weapon, so easy to conceal. He preferred carrying a gun rather than holstering it. What he really wanted to do was take out the AR-15 semi-automatic rifle sitting in the trunk and just put bullets through the entire building—make it clear his objective wasn't coffee and conversation. These kind of low-life traffickers made his skin crawl. He knew he had to keep his emotions in check, stay razor-sharp on the job, get the girl, and get out. He focussed his attention.

2Tall checked his Glock 23 and cloaked it into his pocket, the silencer threaded into place. Cole could feel himself slipping into his armour, heart rate slow and calm, senses heightened, reflexes sharp. They approached the office door, turned the knob slowly, pushed the door open, and walked inside.

The night clerk was tipped back in his chair, ball cap over his eyes, mouth open, with sleep drool running out of the corner of his mouth; feet on the desk, sneaker laces untied, the sole separated from the upper by his big toe on the right foot. He wore a t-shirt with *AC/DC* written on the front, the letters faded from multiple washings, something that clearly hadn't happened in a while, judging from the food stains. His sagging grey track pants matched the food stains on the shirt. Cole and 2Tall stood at the counter. They eyed each other and looked the guy over. Cole kicked the counter, hard. The guy almost fell out of his chair as he jerked awake, hat falling to the floor. He blinked a few times, rubbed his stubble, and stood up.

"Yeah?"

Cole didn't like wasting time. "Where are the girls?"

2Tall folded his fingers around the Glock in his pocket.

The guy stood up. "What?"

"The girls."

The guy yawned and wiped his nose with the back of his hand. "There was only one an…" He stopped, knowing he'd said too much. Cole started walking around the counter.

"You just the night clerk?" 2Tall asked.

"No, I own this dump, who's askin'?" He was wide awake now and sitting up a little taller.

"Where are the girls?"

"Don't know what you're—"

Cole fired a silent shot as he rounded the front desk and got the guy on the side of his left thigh, a flesh wound to get his attention. He screamed and grabbed his leg, looking up at Cole, who now stood over him.

"I'm happy to do the other leg. Wanna answer that question now?"

The guy babbled through his sobs. "It was a new crew.

Never seen them before." He wiped his nose again. "Didn't want no new crew, just more trouble. I told them to go down the road. Tell Alpha I don't want no trouble."

"Where did you send them?" repeated 2Tall.

"Fly High Motel down the road."

Cole and 2Tall turned and started to leave. "What about my fucking leg!" The man yelled at their backs.

Cole turned. "You'll be fine. Get an ice pack and some bandaids. Count your blessings." They walked out to the car and punched the Fly High Motel into the GPS. It was five minutes away. They spun out of the parking lot.

They could see the horizontal orange sign flashing as they sped down the road, getting bigger as they approached, broken lights blinking the name *Fly High Motel*, but the F and T were hidden behind burnt-out bulbs. An airplane balanced on top of the unlit F. Cole killed the headlights and slowed down, rolling onto the side of the road beside the entrance to the motel.

One vehicle was sleepily parked outside unit 14. "There." 2Tall pointed. A guy was leaning against the wall opposite the vehicle, having a smoke, looking at his phone. Empty pizza boxes sat beside him.

Cole stopped the car and turned off the ignition.

They slid out of their seats, staying low, leaving the doors partially open. The interior lights and open door alert had been silenced; the car sat quietly waiting. 2Tall slithered around to the driver's side. They squatted down together. "We'll move to the office, about a hundred yards," said Cole. "I'll wait one minute for you to circle the building and come from the other side. When I see you, we'll move."

"Casualties?" 2Tall asked.

"As many as needed. I'll confirm no civilians are present. That girl will be in our car when we leave in ten minutes."

They both checked their guns and made sure they had two extra magazines. They looked at each other and nodded.

Cole pointed forward with two fingers. They made their move, slick and soundless, like eels in the ocean.

2Tall headed for the side of the building, Glock in hand, then disappeared behind it. Cole crouched and invisibly appeared outside the office. He noticed the clerk was wearing headphones and playing a video game, his back to the window. He'd be there for hours. Cole slid into the shadows along the front of the building and waited for 2Tall. There were no lights in any other room, just 14 where the guy was smoking. Cole was close enough to smell the tobacco. 2Tall rounded the end of the building and signalled. They moved toward the smoker simultaneously. Then the smoker's peripheral vision saw a movement to his left. He pulled his CZ P10 from his pocket and turned toward 2Tall just as Cole shot him in the right thigh. *Clearly not a civilian*, thought Cole. *We're clear.*

The smoker writhed in pain, dropping his gun. Cole moved close enough to see his face just before the guy dove toward the vehicle in front of him, crawling underneath. Cole had seen this guy before. He stopped his brain from searching for intel on the guy, that was for later; this job wasn't finished. 2Tall lunged forward, grabbed the guy's weapon from the ground, pushed the recesses on the sides of the magazine base, and extracted the bullet casings. He threw the gun into the parking lot. Then he fired a shot into each back tire of the vehicle where the guy was cowering. He leaned down, eye to eye with the smoker under the vehicle. He reached in, quick as a cobra, grabbed the guy by the hair, and dragged him along the gravel so his head was exposed just enough. 2Tall lowered his fist into the side of his head, knocking him out cold. He didn't want him dead, he wanted him to tell his gang about this later, he wanted things stirred up. Dead guys couldn't do that. With two strides, 2Tall was back on the sidewalk by the building.

Cole and 2Tall stood on either side of the door where number 14 was imprinted. Cole gave a nod. 2Tall smashed through the door with Cole right behind him. Before the thugs could organize their brains and their guns, Cole fired a shot into the shoulder and leg of the Hawaiian shirt, knocking him flying back into the wall. He slid down, leaving a smear of blood as he collapsed into a pile. 2Tall disabled the right hand and foot of the other thug and then, using the butt of his gun, popped him in the head; he folded into a heap of skin on the floor.

Hailey was lying limp on the bed. Cole quickly scanned the room for any other participants. Silence. He scooped the girl into his arms, cradling her as he ran for the Jeep.

"Is she breathing?" 2Tall asked.

"Barely. Needle marks on her arm."

2Tall raced ahead, popped the trunk, opened the kit Bob had given them, and grabbed the syringe pre-loaded with naloxone.

"Come on, keep breathing," said Cole as he stood at the back of the Jeep, holding Hailey while 2Tall injected the opioid treatment into the muscle of her upper arm. If she didn't respond, there was one shot left in the kit. 2Tall pretzeled himself into the back seat, and Cole placed Hailey into his lap.

"Keep her head up. Let me know if she stops breathing, and I'll stop to give her that last shot."

"Drive." There was an urgency in 2Tall's voice, uncharacteristic of him.

Cole sped down the QEW East. Hailey was breathing—soft and shallow but breathing. Cole knew he had to get out of Niagara. Too many eyes and ears would be active now. He had to get to Toronto. At that hour and at high speed, he calculated he could be in Toronto's west end just shy of an hour. In the event of an emergency, he knew there were other hospitals along the way. Hailey was breathing. He knew they'd get her there in time.

He called Trish on the secure line. "Alert St. Joseph's Health Centre at the west end of Toronto, heroin overdose, there in one hour, less if possible. Update Doc."

As Cole raced across the Skyway Bridge outside Hamilton, a white van whizzed by, going the opposite direction, west. They were the only vehicles on the highway at that time of the morning; it couldn't be coincidence. He was grateful that Trish had installed the state of the art dash cam into her vehicle. He was confident it would capture the van's license plate number. He had a feeling its destination was unit 14 at the Fly High Motel.

NIAGARA FALLS, ONTARIO, CANADA

Misha walked into unit 14.

There was blood everywhere.

Leonard was lying in a ball on the bed, clutching his thigh. His face was blue and swollen.

The other two were on the floor.

All six eyes looked up, pleading for some help as Misha moved into the room.

"What the fuck…" were the first words out of Misha's mouth. Then he pulled out his phone and called their leader. He asked one question, listened, and hung up.

He pulled out his gun and put a bullet in the brain of each guy on the floor. He then ripped the pillowcase and tied it around the top of Leonard's thigh. He screamed.

"Shut the fuck up, you moron," yelled Misha. "That'll stop the bleeding. Get up." Leonard just lay there. Misha kicked the bed. "Get the fuck up, asshole. Help me carry these bodies out to the van. We need to dump them on our turf, not here. We don't need more heat. GET UP!" Misha leaned over, grabbed Leonard by the shirt, and yanked him to his feet.

Leonard screamed again. Blood oozed down his leg. He limped over and picked up the feet of Hawaiian shirt. They carried him out to the van, slowly, since Leonard had to drag his one leg. Once the second body was loaded,

Leonard collapsed into the passenger seat. Misha went back and pulled all the bedding off, stashing it in the back of the van. He wiped down Leonard's car, wiped down the room, closed the door to unit 14, climbed into the driver's seat, and pulled out onto the highway.

"I need to go to a hospital," moaned Leonard.

"Well, that ain't happening, man." Leonard took a breath to protest, but Misha cut him off. "Think about it, man. Think. There are two dead bodies in the back. You have a gunshot wound. We can't stop at a fucking hospital."

"Mish, I won't make it."

"You will. Open the glove box." A mickey of scotch sat waiting and a vial of white powder. Leonard put it to his lips and drained it, then snorted the powder up his nose.

"We'll be back in a couple of hours. The doctor will be waiting there. Get some shuteye. When you wake up, you'll be taken care of. That I can promise you."

Leonard closed his eyes, the drugs and booze and blood loss kicking in.

Back at the Fly High Motel, the clerk adjusted his headphones. The slowly rising sun peeked over the horizon and put a glare on his screen. He leaned forward and turned the television slightly, away from the sun and the reflection, allowing him to finish the video game before his night shift was over.

ST. JOSEPH'S HOSPITAL, TORONTO, CANADA

Cole and 2Tall sat on hard grey plastic chairs, thirty centimetres apart, all screwed onto a metal bar secured into the tiled floor at St. Joe's hospital. They sipped lukewarm coffee that tasted like weak dishwater out of small manila-coloured paper cups. They heard the calls for doctors on the P.A. system, listened to footsteps echo through the pale pink halls, registered the ding of the elevator arriving, the doors opening and closing, the smell of pharmaceuticals, green scrubs, and bleach. The medical team had said they arrived just in time. Now they waited as the staff worked on Hailey. As Cole brought the paper cup to his lips, he saw Mac coming down the hall. He waved. She nodded and continued toward him. Everyone in the hospital seemed to walk with hesitation, as if a disease was lurking and they had to be wary; it added to the hushed atmosphere. Cole stood as Mac approached and hugged her. 2Tall did the same.

"So?" she said.

"We got her here in time. I think she'll be okay," Cole said.

"Oh, thank god," said Mac, sitting down beside Cole. "Jim is on a flight back. Wheels down later today. They'll chopper him over here."

"Won't be easy for him to see her like this," 2Tall said.

"Easier than in the morgue," said Cole. Everyone sat, looking at the floor. "Coffee, Mac?"

"No, I'm good." Mac drew in a long breath. "He'll want to kill those guys who took her."

"Or ask why we didn't," 2Tall said.

"We don't kill unless absolutely necessary… or I give the order," said Cole. "They are just the tentacles. It would have served no purpose to kill them. We need to cut off the head."

"Jim will want a part in that, you know that, right?" Mac said.

"His job is to be with his daughter now. We'll deal with the serpents. You will have to tell him that, Mac. You know he can't be involved."

"That won't be an easy sell," she said.

"He can't snoop around, Mac," 2Tall said.

"I know. I know. I'll talk with him. Any chance he could be involved in some way?"

Cole sipped his dishwater. "Possibly. But we have to do some digging first. We have some leads, but we really don't know much yet, and having Jim breathing down our necks won't speed things up."

"Yeah, you're right, I hear you," Mac said.

"But listen, I get it, I really do. If it were my daughter, I'd want to carve out that pound of flesh myself too. But we have to do this right. Jim knows that. Appeal to the military man, not the dad. And when we have a plan and a potential place for Jim, we will let him know right away. Okay?"

"That's fair. More than fair, actually."

They all looked up as the doctor approached. He looked fatigued. They stood to greet him.

"She's a tough girl. We were able to stabilize her. Giving her naloxone probably saved her life. It is an opioid antagonist, which means that it attaches to opioid receptors and reverses and blocks the drug's effects. We gave her another dose. There was a substantial amount of heroin in her body. She's stable now in the ICU. There will be a recovery period, but she should physically recover. Emotionally, she will need support."

"Her father will be here this afternoon. Will he be able to see her?" Mac asked.

"I am hopeful that by then she will be awake. So, I'll say a tentative yes."

"She's not in danger now, correct?" Cole said.

"Correct. Timing was everything."

They all nodded and shook hands. The doctor turned and left. Cole hugged Mac again. "I'll see you soon."

"Hope so." And she gave him a wink.

"You going to wait here for Jim?"

"I'll go and get some breakfast and come back. Yeah, I'll wait. I think his mom and dad and Abby are on their way. I want to be here when they arrive too."

"I have to go and get things going with the team. 2Tall you stay here, just in case there are thugs trying to pay a visit. I'll let you know when you're needed," Cole said.

"Got it," said 2Tall.

Cole walked over and kissed Mac full on the mouth, then stood back and smiled. Her hand lingered on his arm, and then he turned and walked down the hall toward to exit doors.

"Call Trish," Cole called back to 2Tall. "Let her know I'm on my way, and I have questions."

"Copy that."

Mac and 2Tall walked over to where Hailey was lying in a bed, hooked up to machines. 2Tall pulled over a chair and sat down. "Guess I better get comfortable," he said.

"Want me to bring you some breakfast back?" asked Mac.

"A breakfast sandwich and some decent coffee would be fantastic."

"Done." Mac turned to leave as 2Tall leaned his head back against the wall and rested his eyes.

OTTAWA, ONTARIO, CANADA

The minister of justice went over her brief again. She would soon be addressing a national law enforcement conference, explaining a new bill on the table giving police greater freedom in dealing with crime organizations that target youth. It was a large umbrella, but it was a start. Something she was passionate about. Natalie Sokol was hoping to make an impact and get a large amount of support, which would make passing this bill much easier. At 42, she was one of the younger ministers in cabinet and a woman, so she always had something to prove. She tucked a loose strand of light brown hair behind her ear and looked up over her glasses as her assistant tapped on her door, opened it, and peeked around the corner.

"Yes?"

"Pardon the interruption, Minister, but your husband is here to see you."

"What?" Natalie drew in a long, shaky breath. "Fine, send him in."

As her husband walked into her office and closed the door behind him, her teeth clenched slightly. "What the hell are you doing here?"

"Nice to see you too, Nat."

"What are you doing here?"

"Miranda thought you might be able to come to the

tournament that's happening at my club. She'll be playing. It's coming up soon. I said I'd ask."

"You could ask that on the phone. Plus, she's a big girl. She could ask me herself."

"Yes, I am aware of that. I said I would ask. So I'm asking."

"What are you asking?"

"If you're coming."

"And why exactly are you asking at all?"

"I told you, I said I would."

Natalie stood, statue-like, waiting.

"You're going to squash that new bill you're proposing." Sokol spoke with a cobra-like coil.

"What?"

"Stop the bill. It will dent my business."

"What business, the golf course?"

"The trucking business."

"How is transporting military furniture going to be affected by a law to protect minors?"

"It will make everything more difficult, more paperwork, more headaches. I don't want more headaches."

"I can't do that."

"Oh yes, you can and you will. That's our agreement. I didn't pay for your education and campaign funds so you could just fuck me and my business when you want to. What do you—"

"I should never have taken your goddamn money," she said, almost under her breath.

"What is that supposed to mean?"

"I think what I said was pretty clear, even for an idiot."

"You calling me an idiot?"

"Well, you know what they say, if the sh—"

"Shut the fuck up and do as you are told."

"I have a commitment to my constituents and—"

"No, no, my girl. Your commitment is to me first. Period. You know—"

"It's your company, not mine."

"Yes, it is mine, and I won't have you ruin what I've built."

"No, Andrej. This bill has nothing to do with your company. I don't know what you are talking about or why you are so concerned. No."

Sokol's face was turning red, his fists clenched. He looked her in the eye, then slapped her hard across the face, leaving red finger marks and a thin trail of blood where his fingernail punctured her skin.

Her hand flew to her cheek, tears of rage stinging her eyes. She pulled her hand back, looking at the blood. She reached for a tissue on her desk, dabbing it onto her cheekbone just below her eye, collecting the blood. "Okay, okay," she whispered through her teeth. "I'll see what I can do. Fine." Her face was bruising, she could feel the swelling. She needed ice. Her mind raced to create a reason why her face would soon be red and swollen. But she was good at creating stories. Sokol had given her lots of practice.

"Make it go away, Natalie."

"Get out."

"So, are you coming to the tournament? For our daughter?"

"Don't pretend to care. Give the dates to my assistant, and I'll arrange to be there on the final day. For Miranda."

"There, now, was all that so hard?"

"Get out of my office."

Sokol put his hand on the doorknob. "Make it happen, Natalie. We have an agreement." He flashed a sociopathic kind of smile in her direction and walked out the door.

Natalie Sokol collapsed into her chair and leaned back, looking up at the ceiling, hoping to find the answer there on how to make her life less splintered. How to make her life whole. She buzzed her assistant.

"Could you bring me a glass of water with lots of ice?"

ST. JOSEPH'S HOSPITAL, TORONTO, CANADA

Jim pulled up a chair next to his daughter's bed, sat down, and took her hand in his. The starched white sheets were folded perfectly, a thin grey blanket rested on top. Her hands were neatly placed alongside her body. The top of her bed was cranked to a forty-five-degree angle, a stiff white pillow beneath her head. She lay unmoving except for the shallow rise and fall of her chest. Her slender body formed impressions in the blanket the way objects become covered with a falling snow and still hold their shape. The room held a listless and empty feeling. Sanitized. Cold. All the blood and carnage and killing Jim had witnessed didn't hold a candle to seeing his daughter lying in that hospital bed, IVs in her arm, damp and limp hair stuck to her forehead, eyes closed. The *beep-beep* of the machines moved his mind back to when he was sitting holding his wife's hand, knowing they wouldn't be walking out of the hospital together, knowing it would be her last smile, the last warmth of her skin, the last time her eyes would pull him in and wrap him up like no one else could. He moved the hair from Hailey's cheek. She looked so much like Helen. He felt warm, salty water filling his eyes. The doctor said Hailey would fully recover. She'd just need time. The emotional scars were the biggest concern. But first, they needed to get her home.

Jim saw a flutter underneath her eyelids. Slowly, like the curtain rising on an opening night production, her eyes began to open.

Tears spilled over onto Jim's cheeks.

"Dad?"

"I'm here, honey. I'm here."

She squeezed his hand and closed her eyes again.

There was a knock on the door. Jim turned his head.

"Sorry to interrupt, Captain. A word?"

Jim stood, the feet of his chair scraping on the tiled floor as it pushed back. He leaned over and kissed his daughter on the forehead. Her eyes opened wide, and there was a flash of panic across her face.

"It's okay. You're safe. I'll just be outside the door."

Her eyes followed him to the door, then closed again.

Jim gently closed the door and stood facing a heavy-set man. He had an air of authority about him. He was dressed in a dark suit and dark tie with tiny white dots against a starched shirt with thin blue lines. His neck bulged slightly above the button fastened at the top of his collar. His head was buzzed, and he had a shadow of a beard. He extended his hand. The whites of his eyes were as piercing as the black of his irises.

"Detective Sergeant Jones."

Jim brought up his tanned yet white hand and met the grip of the darker-skinned hand. The two men shook firmly.

"There is no way you are going to talk to my daughter right now."

"Understood. No need."

"What then?"

"Bill Thornton contacted me. We go way back. Worked a number of undercover operations together. Let's just say we both owe each other. He's called in a favour. He said he and Cole Buckman want to keep this situation off the books for as long as possible. No police intervention."

"Thank you."

"Because Bill asked, the hospital has been told I am handling it, and no one else is to be told or contacted. They are to call me directly if there are any inquiries about the situation. Bill says they feel this goes much deeper than what happened with your daughter…"

"And if police are involved," interjected Jim, "all the rats will run back into their holes."

"Exactly. And we want all the rats. Not just a few. Especially the rat king."

"Do you have authorization to keep things that quiet?" asked Jim.

"A few years ago I became part of CSO."

"CSO?"

"If you haven't been pulled in to do an op with the team, you may not be aware it even exists. CSO is Canadian Special Operations team. We combine powers of military, RCMP, and CSIS. The CSO team seconded me from police services. It was an opportunity for sure."

"That's a lot of clout right there. How long are you willing to keep things quiet? How long will you be able to keep things quiet."

"I have my ways. Bill called in a favour. So I'll wait until he contacts me. He'll let me know how their investigation is going. They've already started. Best not to muddy those waters."

Jim stood, his hand at his sides, his fists clenching and unclenching. "When you say 'their,' are you meaning Cole and his team?"

"I am."

"Yeah, they have started. You're right, let it play out. Muddying the waters could ruin the whole thing."

"Not my first rodeo. I know when to stand back. And I trust Bill. But more than anything, I want these pricks too."

"Me too. Fuck, I want those bastards."

"And that's why you are leaving this to Cole and his team."

"What do you mean?"

"Would you allow anyone into an op if they were as charged with emotion as you are right now?"

"No. Point taken." Jim took a deep breath.

"How is your daughter doing?" asked Jones.

"She's alive. Breathing on her own. We're hoping for a full recovery."

"That's good news."

Jim nodded his head in agreement. "Get those sons of bitches."

"That's the plan."

"Thanks again."

"It's what we do."

Jim reached his hand out. They shook, nodded, and Jones turned to leave. Jim stood for a moment, collecting his thoughts and his emotions. A slow smile crept across his face as a familiar cadence of military issued boots made their way down the hall toward him. He looked up. "Mac," he said warmly. She moved in for a hug. They stood like that for a few seconds; Jim didn't realize how much he had needed that comfort.

She stepped back, put her hands on his shoulders, and looked at him. "She's going to be okay, Jim."

"Yes, so they say. Any leads on these guys? Jones said he's leaving it to Cole and his team."

"Cole and his team are on it. They saved her life, Jim. They've got this. 2Tall is going to stay at the hospital until she goes home." She pointed in the direction of the nurses' station, and 2Tall sitting in a chair, legs crossed, waved when he saw them looking in his direction. "When you aren't in the room, he will be.

Cole is taking every precaution."

"I want these guys."

"I know. We all do. But you have to stay out of this." Jim's eyes widened. "I'm serious, Jim. Cole will let me know when he feels you can be pulled in. Meantime, look after your daughter. No one can replace you as a dad. Cole and his team will handle whoever did this."

"Okay. I get it. Jones just told me the same thing."

"I need your word, Jim."

Jim stood for a long minute. Time seemed to hover. He glanced at the door leading into the room where his daughter lay and then looked back to Mac. "You have my word."

"Good. Will you be here for a while?"

"Yes. I've taken leave."

"How long?"

"Until further notice."

"I'm glad to hear it. Your family needs you."

Jim took a deep breath. "I know."

"Speak of the devil," said Mac, and she pointed down the hall. Abby saw her dad and ran ahead. Grammy and Grandpa Morrison followed behind. They all hugged.

"Where is she?" asked Grammy Morrison.

Jim indicated with a tilt of his head. "Are the other girls safe?"

"Yes, they are on their way home with their parents

now," said Grandpa Morrison.

"Can we see her, Dad?"

"We can only go in one at a time."

"When will she come home?" asked Grammy Morrison.

"I'm bringing her home tomorrow. She's recovering quickly."

"Will you be staying?" asked Abby.

He put his arm around his oldest daughter and pulled her in close. He kissed the top of her head. "I will, honey. I'm going to be home for a while now."

"I'm going in to see Hailey." Grammy Morrison gently opened the door and moved inside.

Mac squeezed Jim's arm and stepped to one side, letting the family support each other. There was work to do. She sent Cole a text letting him know everything was in place.

TORONTO HARBOUR, ONTARIO, CANADA

Trish was sorting through a stack of mail she'd picked up from Cole's condo. "Hey Cole, have you been back to your condo recently?"

"Come to think of it, no."

"Good that I pop over once in a while," she said, waving handfuls of envelopes in the air. "This is quite the stack of unopened mail."

"Yeah, sorry about that. Thanks for grabbing it. Anything interesting?"

She held up an envelope.

"What is it?" Charlie asked.

"Appears to be from a golf club." Trish proceeded to rip open the envelope, pulling out an invitation. She smiled and looked up.

"Okay, why that smile?" Bill asked.

"Remember that golfer, Miranda Sokol?"

"The one who has the hots for Cole?"

"That's the one. Cole is invited to a mixed tournament and is paired up with Miranda."

"What kind of tournament?" Cole asked.

"Probably one where you hit that little dimpled white ball with a really big club," Bill said. They all laughed.

"Very funny. Ha ha," Cole said.

"There's a big purse," said Trish. "Big players are

showing up from PGA and LPGA. Always good to do one of those, Cole. Keep your cover intact."

"When is it?"

"This weekend," she said.

"Kind of short notice," Cole said.

"The postmark is months ago," Trish said.

"Oh."

"Where is the club again?" Charlie asked.

"Kingston," Trish said.

"Curious. I was doing a little digging into that license plate you sent us, Cole, the one on that white van," said Charlie. "Turns out it's registered to a numbered company. And as I couldn't find out any other details with my limited computer skills…"

"…he handed it to me," said Trish.

"What does this have to do with the golf tournament?" Bill asked.

"Well, when I did some under-the-covers digging, I found that the address of the company is located in Brockville, just a stone's throw from where the tournament is being held in Kingston."

"So while Cole plays and you caddy, I can go and do a little digging of my own," Bill said.

"Exactly," Charlie said. "And, seeing as we'll be in Kingston, I can have lunch with Cynthia. Haven't seen her in a while." He glanced over at Trish, who quietly smiled.

"Trish, see if I can still be paired up. They may have all their players already," Cole said.

"True, but if Miranda wants you there, she'll replace her partner with you lickety-split." Trish winked. Everyone else smiled.

"Do your magic, Trish," Cole said. "Bill, you hold up here. Charlie, you do some snooping in Brockville, after a nice dinner with Cynthia. How is she doing?"

"Good. Good. We keep in touch, but I haven't seen her in a while. I'll give her a call," said Charlie. "Any update on Hailey?"

"She's doing well. Jim is taking her home tomorrow, so 2Tall will be back."

"I'm sure Jim's looking for a little blood," Bill said.

"I'd say a lot of blood," Trish added.

"That could be a problem. I've left it with Mac," Cole said.

"Left what with Mac?" Charlie asked.

"Keeping Jim restrained."

"Oh, good idea," said Trish. "But he could be an asset in tracking these guys down, you know."

"Yeah, I thought that too," Cole said. "Let's see where things lead, and we'll pull him in if it looks doable. Trish, let 2Tall know we'll need him at the golf course in Kingston. He should go there right from the hospital. Give him the hotel info."

"On it."

Bill rummaged around in the mail Trish had dropped onto the table. He pulled out a postcard and lifted it up. "A sandy beach in Cuba. Looks like Kitch knows how to take a vacation."

"Since when does your dad take a vacation, Cole?" Charlie said.

"Since almost dying on our last mission."

"Yeah, good reason," said Bill. "Why aren't we there too?"

KINGSTON, ONTARIO, CANADA

"My birthday isn't for another month, Charlie," said Cynthia, her arm looped through his as he guided her to the front doors of Bistro Miguel, her favourite restaurant.

"I am well aware of that, but I was in town this weekend and thought it would be nice to get together, because I always love getting together with you."

Cynthia blushed and gripped his arm as a lover squeezes a hand to reinforce emotion. Butterflies danced in her stomach. She knew she loved Charlie. She always had, and time had softened her wounds so that those feelings had been able to rise to the surface more and more. She wondered if he felt the same, or was she just a friend?

He stopped in front of two stairs. "Step," he said. "Two, in fact." She lifted her foot, felt the pressure of the step, and stepped again.

"Thank you," she said.

He smiled, and although she couldn't see it, she could feel it. He opened the door, and they walked inside.

"Good evening. Reservation, sir?"

"Yes. Foster."

The hostess checked her book and picked up two menus. "Right this way, sir."

Cynthia was happy to hold Charlie's hand a bit longer as they followed the hostess to their favourite table.

Cynthia loved to feel the sun on her face if she was there for lunch, and it was an easy walk to the ladies' room. A large stone fireplace accented the wall from floor to ceiling, with a thick cedar beam set into the centre. It was a cool evening, and a fire was gently smouldering. The rest of the walls were painted a warm honey colour, adorned with art created by local artists. Tall plants sat in corners, their wide, succulent leaves inviting tranquility. It always pained Charlie that Cynthia couldn't see how beautifully the place was decorated. But she always said she could feel the good energy of a place. A sole musician played baroque music on her classical guitar, notes floating between tables as Charlie helped Cynthia into her chair. Her hands found the table and gingerly felt around for all the items in front of her.

"Hmm, my favourite table. I can smell the fire, hear it crackling. Thank you, Charlie. You really didn't have to."

"Of course I did," he said, settling into his own chair. "You are one of my very favourite people."

"You're smiling now, aren't you?" she said.

"Yes, yes I am." Her hand was on the table, and he reached over, covering it with his own. She didn't resist. And so he took a chance and gently pulled her hand into his, wrapping it in his fingers. She squeezed back. Charlie leaned forward, lifted her hand to his lips, and kissed it. A tear escaped her eye and found its way down her cheek.

He leaned over and gently wiped it away.

"Why are you crying? Have I offended you?"

"No, just the opposite. I wasn't sure if we were just friends."

"I was thinking the same thing. Would you be happy if it was more?" He held his breath, waiting for the answer.

"Charlie, I know I pushed you away, for years, really. But I have never stopped loving you. And now, well, I'm okay, I'm better than okay, and my feelings for you are bubbling to the surface." She was blushing again.

"Cynthia, I have never stopped loving you either. But I never wanted to push you."

"I know. And I thank you so much."

Charlie was a little choked up. He hadn't been expecting this kind of evening. His heart raced, and he wanted to jump onto the table and dance a jig. Maybe it really was going to all be okay after all.

"Would you like me to read you the specials on the board? Order some wine?"

"Perfect."

"And I know your favourite wine."

"You always do."

Charlie began to read the appetizer selection when Cynthia interrupted him. "Charlie, what is the commotion, somewhere behind me?"

Charlie leaned to one side, peering into the adjoining

room. "A few people are taking photos, oh wait, I see…"

"What, who is it?"

"Not really sure. I'm not the guy to ask about celebrities." They both laughed. "Looks like a well known couple is out for dinner. It's only the two of them, so he is either her husband or her brother."

"Or a lover."

"Oooh, juicy. If that's true, the press will have a field day with these photos… depending on how famous they are."

They both laughed.

"The duck *à l'orange* is on the board tonight, Cyn."

"Oh, I can never resist that."

"Maybe some stuffed mushrooms to start with your wine?"

"Sounds perfect. Charlie?"

"Yes. Yes, it does." He squeezed her hand.

"Is there a server? I'd just like to visit the little girl's room."

Charlie surveyed the room, catching the eye of one of the servers and waving her over. He pushed his chair back and went over to Cynthia, handing her the white cane as she stood up. "Cynthia, I…" But before he could finish, her hand had found his cheek, and her lips had found his. To Charlie, their kiss lasted an eternity, a kiss that he been waiting for, imagining, for too many years. The waitress stood patiently beside Charlie, smiling as one does when watching a heartfelt rom com. He reluctantly finished their kiss, wishing they were not in such a public place, and stood back, glowing inside.

"Sir, your server will be with you shortly," said the waitress. "I am not serving this section."

"Yes, I understand, but my friend needs to use the bathroom. Could you please provide some assistance to her?"

The server saw the white cane in Cynthia's hand. "Of course." She put Cynthia's arm on hers and led her to the ladies' room.

Charlie returned to his seat, warm and tingly with the knowledge that Cynthia returned his love. After all this time, he couldn't quite believe it. Maybe he should have made a move earlier… but no, it all seemed to be falling into place. He hadn't felt so happy in a very, very long time. He reluctantly checked his phone as the waiter came to the table, and Charlie gave him their order. When he looked back down at his phone, he saw a text from Cole saying all was proceeding well. They would all meet when *Windy Girl* was in port. Charlie sent an affirmative reply as the waiter returned with the bottle of wine and began to fill each wine glass. When Cynthia returned to the table and was settled into her chair, Charlie noticed she seemed a little flushed.

"Is everything okay, Cyn?"

Cynthia sat quietly, her face a bit pale. Charlie reached over and put his hand on hers. "Cynthia, what is it? What's happened?" He could see she was struggling not to cry. He put a napkin into her hand.

"As I was coming back from the restroom, I heard a conversation…"

"Okay, there are a lot of conversations happening here…"

"Charlie, it was his voice."

"Whose voice? What are you talking about?"

"The voice I will never ever get out of my head."

Charlie became rigid. "The voice from that night all those years ago?"

"Yes," Cynthia almost whispered.

"Holy fuck. Are you sure?"

"Absolutely."

"Who? Where is he?"

"I think it's where all the commotion was coming from. And whoever it is sounds angry, that same angry from that night."

He slid Cynthia's hand to her goblet. "Here, have some wine."

She lifted the wine glass and took a long sip. "This wine is so delicious, Charlie. But… I don't know if I can stay now."

"It looks like they are getting ready to leave. Let's not let anyone take away this evening from us." He put his hand on hers, and she nodded in agreement. "Why don't you sip your wine and just gather yourself, breathe. I'm going to quickly visit the washroom myself."

Charlie walked away from the table while selecting the video option from his phone camera. As other people were taking photos, his phone wouldn't stand out. But he didn't just want a photo; he wanted to catch their voices as well. He tuned into conversations in that area of the room, trying to focus on an angry voice. Since most people were there for a lovely evening out and appeared happy and content, he didn't think that would be hard to find. And then he heard it; an impatient, angry tone. He slowly turned his head to see a man holding a jacket for a woman; he was clearly admonishing her for something. People were madly taking pictures, and so Charlie quickly lifted up his phone and hit *record*. Even though the couple was clearly fighting, they had well practiced smiles pasted to their faces; they were obviously used to being photographed. He wished he knew who they were. But it didn't matter. He had it all on his phone. The man was now ushering the woman between tables and heading for the door. Charlie turned and went back to his table.

"They have left. I got a photo and a video. I'll show it to Trish and Cole. Then we'll have some answers."

"Okay, Charlie. Thanks. Again." She put on a small smile. "You're always there for me."

"And I always will be."

"I know. And I love that."

Charlie was blushing now. "Madam, can I refill your glass?"

"Thank you, kind sir, that would be lovely. The wine is divine."

"As are you."

"You're so sweet. And you're right, Charlie, we won't let anyone take time away from us again. To us."

And she lifted her glass, which he happily met with his own.

EASTERN RIDGE GOLF AND COUNTRY CLUB, KINGSTON, ONTARIO, CANADA

It was a flurry of activity, colour, clothes, caddies, carts, and celebrities. It was opening day of the Eastern Ridge Golf and Country Club's Mixed Professional Tournament, and anticipation was in the air. Andrej Sokol had pulled out all the stops to impress. Brooke Henderson and Lexi Thompson were chatting as they waited for their group to gather. Jon Rahm and Jordan Speith were getting ready to tee off. Cole stood talking with Trish, who was caddying for him. She wore lime-green slacks and a white golf shirt, her hair tied back into a ponytail. She looked stunning. Miranda Sokol took in her every inch. She wasn't at all impressed that Cole's caddy was so hot. She undid one more button on her pink polka-dotted golf shirt and adjusted her shorter than usual pink skort. She went and stood unnecessarily close to Cole under the guise of collaboration, moving between him and his caddy. Trish smiled, winked at Cole, and retreated to the golf bag. She'd been right about Miranda; the minute she'd found out Cole wanted to come, she orchestrated a change in partner. It seemed her dad was happy to oblige his daughter, even though a number of people had walked away pissed.

The tournament's format dictated that they would play

two rounds, the same as the last two days of a Masters tournament. The grounds were abuzz with anticipatory energy. Crowds had already lined up behind the ropes and filled the seats in the stands surrounding hole one and hole eighteen as the first few teams teed off. The tournament was underway.

Cole was gently swinging his driver from side to side, warming up; Miranda was adjusting her glove, glancing at him from the corner of her eye. She went and stood beside Cole. "Do we have any strategy?" she asked.

"Get the little ball in the hole as quickly as possible."

She forced a laugh. "Who should tee off first?"

"Well, what would make you more comfortable? We have to stay liquid."

She gave him a warm smile. "I'll start."

It was their turn. As they moved forward and into the tee box, they were announced over the loudspeaker. The crowd cheered, knowing Miranda was a local girl. Cole could see she was nervous. Always more pressure on home turf. He leaned over to her as she took her driver from her caddy. "You've got this, partner." Miranda's face remained stoic and focused, but her heart was racing.

They both hit a solid drive, but as they proceeded down the fairway, Cole could see that Miranda was still eyeing Trish. He talked with Miranda as they walked down the fairway, telling her to focus on the game, focus on her next shot. By the ninth hole, they had both found their rhythm and were in second place on the leaderboard behind Speith and Henderson.

As they approached the tenth hole, a par three, Miranda offered Cole a strategy. She knew this course well. She knew she couldn't quite make the green from the tee box, but she was pretty sure that Cole would. If he played the hole on his own, they would score higher if he birdied. He agreed to play the hole without her.

He moved in to address the ball. He held a five-iron in his hand, slowly brought the club back, and then powerfully connected with the ball. It landed inches from the hole; one putt for a birdie would put them into the lead. Miranda and Cole high-fived as they walked toward the green. Cole easily sank his ball: they were first on the leader board now. Their luck continued, and the crowd following them began to grow.

By hole eighteen they had a two-stroke lead over Henderson and Speith, hot on their heels. After hitting a fantastic drive out of the tee box, Miranda walked up to her ball on the fairway, perfectly placed. She talked with her caddy and decided on the seven-iron. The ball sailed toward the green. The crowd started to cheer as it got closer and closer, heading for an eagle. Everyone thought it was going to go in. The energy was electric, but it hit the pin, dropping a few feet away. She put a birdie in the hole.

They were three shots ahead as the last team walked off the course.

It had been a good day. Trish was happily sitting with her feet up on the patio with a drink in her hand, debriefing with the other caddies. Cole was walking through the clubhouse on his way to the locker room. As he turned a corner he saw a man, not a golfer, but he knew that face. He watched him go into an office. The recognition software in Cole's head jumped into motion, searching for the face until… there it was. He was the guy he'd shot outside room fourteen at Fly High Motel. What the fuck was he doing here? Cole's skin began to prickle. He walked toward the room the man had entered, Andrej Sokol's name was secured on the door with in a bronze plaque, but before he could turn the handle and confront him, there was a warm hand on his shoulder and a soft voice in his ear.

"Follow me," she said. "I want to show you something." The hand slid down his arm from his shoulder, grasping his hand in a firm grip. Miranda moved past Cole, holding his hand, pulling him forward with her. She turned the door handle. Cole was expecting to be confronted by the man who had just entered, but as they stepped into the room, it was empty. Cole was perplexed, surveying the room. Nothing. No one. And no hiding places. The room was sparsely furnished and neat as a pin. There was no other exit. Which left only one option: there was a secret room with a seamless entrance.

Miranda closed the door, secured the lock into place, turned to Cole, and proceeded to kiss him on the mouth as her arms went around his neck, her body pressing into his. Cole untangled his thoughts quickly. He put his hands onto Miranda's arms and gently stepped back, out of the kiss. He smiled kindly, his brain racing for a safety net.

"I'm not sure this is the time and place, Miranda. I mean, we've got a tournament to play and we're doing pretty well. If we continue with this right now, we certainly won't be able to concentrate on our game." He pulled down his shirt and stroked her arm, not wanting a scene.

"I'm sorry. Yes, of course. You're so right. What was I thinking? We can find a place after the tournament is finished."

"Of course. Much better." He kept a straight face.

Miranda stroked his cheek and slid her hand down his arm. "You go out first so we aren't seen coming out together."

"Good idea."

"See you tomorrow, partner." She winked.

Cole smiled and then turned and left the room. Walking down the hall, he sent a text to Trish: *Meet me out front ASAP.*

Trish instantly put down her drink and excused herself from the discussion. Cole was waiting for her on one of the benches out front. She sat down beside him. It would look like a strategy session for the next day of play.

"What's up?"

"Not sure. But something is for sure. We have to get into Sokol's office, tonight."

"Tonight? Why? Can't it wait until after the tournament tomorrow?"

Cole turned and stared at her.

"Right. Tonight it is. I better figure out the security system right now."

Cole smiled and nodded.

"There is a dinner at six," said Trish. "But things won't go late; it's an early start tomorrow."

"Meet me in my hotel room at nine. We'll go over details. Tell 2Tall he'll be on surveillance duty at the golf course tonight. And contact Bill. He needs to sail *Windy Girl* over to Portsmouth Olympic Harbour now. My spidey sense tells me we won't be leaving Kingston too quickly."

SOKOL RESIDENCE, KINGSTON, ONTARIO, CANADA

Miranda walked into her parents' spacious living room and kicked off her shoes. She flopped down on the cream-coloured designer sectional, put her head back, and let out a sigh.

"Long day?"

Miranda sat up quickly. "Mom. You're home." She jumped off the couch and threw her arms around Natalie. "I wasn't expecting you until the end of the tournament."

"I know. I came early. I wanted to see you play tomorrow, and I had dinner with your father last night."

"Ohhhh, how did that go?" They sat down on the couch together. "By that not very well concealed bruise on your face, I'd say it didn't go that well."

"Well, that is from a different day. But the dinner wasn't much better. At least he keeps his hands to himself in public. You know your father."

"Sadly, yes. But Mom, I mean, how long are you going to let this keep happening?"

Natalie leaned back into the couch, sighing. This wasn't the time or place to try to explain the complex and disturbing mess she'd gotten herself into. "Forget about him. Tell me about your day first."

Miranda ignored the question. "I'm surprised you came over here and didn't just go right to your condo."

"Well, you didn't know I was coming into town, I knew you'd be staying here, and I wanted to see you."

"Plus, you like to keep up appearances, and with me here it's a bit safer."

"Something like that, yeah." Natalie pressed her lips together and sighed. She didn't want Miranda more in the middle than she already was. It all turned her stomach. She wished she could think of a way out. But her husband wasn't one to be crossed. She would have to bide her time.

"Come on, tell me about your day. How did it go with Cole?"

Miranda dropped her eyes, blushing ever so slightly, and fiddled with the hem of her dress. "We played really well. He was really helpful and took suggestions I gave him. It was a good day."

"But…"

"Well, I thought he would sit with me at the dinner tonight, but he sat with other players, male players."

"That doesn't seem out of the ordinary."

"I know, it's just…"

"It's just that you'd like him to feel about you the way you feel about him."

Miranda looked at her mom. "Yes."

"And he doesn't."

"No."

"You sure?"

"Pretty sure. There was a moment in Dad's office after we handed our cards in, and, well, it didn't go the way I'd hoped."

"I'm sorry, honey. Will you finish the tournament together?"

"Oh yes. That's business. And playing with him is really great. He's a great golfer."

"Think you could win?"

"Well, Dad sure wants that."

"I bet he does. Winning is his only goal. At everything."

"Yup."

"Anyway, I'll be here for the weekend."

"Oh, that's great. What a nice surprise. Now I'll play even better knowing you're in the crowd. I love having you around." She leaned over and hugged her mom again.

"How about we raid the fridge together?" said Natalie.

"Great idea."

"Is your dad going to be walking in the door soon?"

"Yes, he is. Said he wants to get an early night."

"Well, why don't we get out of here and raid the fridge at my condo? Want to have a sleepover?"

"Pillow fights too?"

"Of course. Will your dad be pissed if you're not here?"

"Won't even notice."

They both laughed.

"Okay, grab some stuff, and let's scram before he gets home."

"I don't need anything. Let's go."

They put their arms around each other and headed for Natalie's car.

EASTERN RIDGE GOLF AND COUNTRY CLUB, KINGSTON, ONTARIO, CANADA

Everyone had left the club after the dinner. Tables had been cleared, floors swept, doors locked, and lights turned off, all around 8:00 p.m. The club was now quietly sleeping until everyone would return at 5:00 a.m. for day two.

Trish had done her job, as usual. She had tapped into the security system of the club, disabling all alarms, cameras, and sensors. 2Tall was parked strategically so he could see the parking lot and the clubhouse from the side and the back. They were all wearing coms.

Dressed in black from head to foot, Cole and Trish approached the clubhouse from the first green, where her Jeep was parked on the gravel road. There were no guards on duty, no houses close by, no moon. It was a dark, black night. Perfect. All three tested out their coms to make sure they were connected. When that was established, Trish and Cole moved stealthily into the black of night shadows, becoming shadows themselves. Trish hovered as the lookout while Cole masterfully picked the lock on the rear entrance. They moved through the halls like underwater divers, and after the third turn, they stood in front of Sokol's office. Cole again picked the lock, and they disappeared into the room. The door closed with a click behind them. No words were spoken; there were probably recording devices in the room.

Cole began to slide his hand along the walls, his fingers seeking a seam or crack. Trish did the same to the outside and underside of Sokol's desk. Her index finger found a small, smooth, round depressed node; she pressed it. Immediately, the wall where Cole was standing jutted forward and slid to the right, revealing an inner chamber. Lights flickered on in the secret room.

Trish came and stood beside Cole. They were looking at a sea of computers, smart boards, computer-generated holography screens and weapons: AK-47s, Tokarev pistols, tommy guns, and even a few RPGs. Loaded thirty-round mags were stacked up in the corner, knee-high. Drums filled with 45acp and crates of 7.62X39 took up even more real estate. Trish and Cole turned their heads and stared into each other's widened eyes.

They worked fast, careful not to disturb anything. They took photos and downloaded info onto a thumb drive from the main computer. Information flashed across screens, and something about a trucking company kept popping up. Cole pointed at a screen, getting Trish's attention. It was large and successful, judging by the financial records. Sokol's name was nowhere in any of the documents, but three other persons were mentioned in a lot of the files: Misha Cerny, Leonard Sitsua, and Katya Nemec.

Trish pressed some keys until destinations/drop sights

for trucks were displayed on the holographic screen. Stops were plotted all along the 401 highway corridor from Toronto to Kingston. What were they transporting? Trish pointed to her screen, getting Cole's attention. Three drivers had recently left, leaving them short for the next pickup delivery. The pickup and delivery was left a mystery. Trish was about to search for more info when Cole put a hand on her shoulder. He put his other hand to his ear. 2Tall was speaking in the coms. "Code red, vehicle has parked outside the clubhouse, driver has exited the vehicle."

Cole motioned to Trish: time to leave. Trish stood and put the flash drive into her pocket. Quickly, they left the chamber, slid the door closed, navigated through the dark halls, and out the back door. They stayed in the trees on the edge of the first green until they reached the Jeep.

"We're out. Mission accomplished."

2Tall pulled away.

Without engaging the headlights, Trish and Cole made their way down the gravel road toward their hotel.

Cole's mind was racing. "We have to get word to the team. Something smells very, very bad."

"Already ahead of you, Cole," said Trish, typing her text to the Wookies.

Back at the clubhouse, Sokol unlocked the office door,

pushed on the wall to open the chamber, and walked inside. He sat down at the computer. Misha had just informed him they were down a few drivers, and the timing couldn't have been worse.

RAMADA INN, KINGSTON, ONTARIO, CANADA

Cole and Trish huddled around the small table in the hotel room, waiting for the team to pick up on their secure lines. They would have to use their handles just in case anyone was listening.

"Did you find anything?" asked Doc, sitting below deck at mission control and making good headway across Lake Ontario.

"A hidden, fully loaded chamber," Falcon said.

"Cool," 2Tall said. "Any intel?"

"Oh yeah. We'll debrief tomorrow. Meantime… Doc, you're going undercover as a driver with a trucking company. Tuna, 2Tall, get all the documents together that he'll need. The tournament's over tomorrow. Be ready by then."

"Copy that," they all answered together.

"Doc," said Cole, "what's *Windy Girl*'s ETA in Kingston?"

"Early tomorrow morning if the wind holds up."

"Forecast?"

"Good."

"We'll convene on *Windy Girl* tomorrow evening. First, we have a tournament to win."

EASTERN RIDGE GOLF COURSE AND COUNTRY CLUB, KINGSTON, ONTARIO, CANADA

A warm sun and a gentle breeze greeted the second and final day of the golf tournament. There were more fans on the final day, and crowds were large. The one new face in the crowd following Cole and Miranda was none other than Natalie Sokol. Miranda wanted to make her proud.

Cole and Miranda were playing well and holding their lead. And then on the twelfth hole, Miranda's drive hooked into the trees, costing her a number of extra strokes. She was devastated. She bogeyed the hole. And on the thirteenth, she dropped her ball into the bunker. Cole could see the wheels coming off the bus. Her face was tense. He calmly walked over to her and put a hand on her shoulder. "Pull yourself together. You're a professional, you can do this. Let's win." She looked back at him. Her face calmed. And on the next par three, she dropped her ball inches from the hole.

Rahm and Thompson moved ahead. But Speith and Henderson were now tied with Cole and Miranda.

Rahm and Thompson bogeyed the eighteenth. It was now down to Speith and Henderson and Buckman and Sokol.

Miranda hit a brilliant drive. Cole didn't disappoint either. It came down to the last few putts. Miranda parred the hole, but Cole's ball found a curve just before the hole and slipped to the side. He was one over.

The tournament went to Rahm and Thompson.

Miranda was noticeably heartbroken. Her mother walked out of the crowd and wrapped her in a big mama hug. Then she turned and shook Cole's hand. Cole was happy with second place. He never wanted to gain more attention than necessary.

Everyone made their way to the clubhouse for drinks, food, speeches, and awards. It had been a good day. Trish was happily sitting with her feet up on the patio with a drink in her hand, debriefing with the other caddies.

In only the past year, Trish had made a name for herself as an up-and-coming professional caddie for the mysterious Cole Buckman. And that just added to the validity of their cover. Cole and Trish were known for breezing in and out of PGA events. And that was good too; it keep everyone guessing.

Of course, no one knew Cole's real identity, and hardly anyone knew Trish was a retired homicide detective, except for Michael Greller, Jordan Speith's longtime caddie and the guy who had mentored Trish. Long before Trish even met Cole and Michael was a math teacher, their paths had crossed and Trish had interviewed Michael as a witness to a crime. When they met on the golf course years later, he just assumed she had changed jobs as he had. Trish never filled in the blanks for him. They were both caddies now, and caddies have a special relationship with the players they work with, often having to convince them to use a certain club or take a directed shot.

Michael had watched Trish gently talk Cole into changing clubs on the course earlier. She did her job well. So, as she now sat with her feet up, Michael pulled a chair up beside her. He was considered one of the best caddies on the tour and had taught Trish a lot; she was constantly receiving offers from other players to join them.

"Nice work out there today," said Michael.

"Thanks, you too."

"Hard keeping those golfer egos in check sometimes."

"Sometimes?" Trish laughed.

"Very true. Not so much helping them with what club, but more remembering we are just hitting a little white ball on nicely cut grass."

"Yeah, a ball worth millions of dollars," Brittany Henderson interjected and pulled up a chair. She was Brook Henderson's older sister and caddie. "How did you get Cole to change that club on hole seven today?" she asked Trish.

"Well, Brittany, I just took a page out of your book… slow and steady and try not to rock the ego boat too much."

"It's a fine line," said Michael. "They need to listen because they often get lost in their own world, but they need to believe in themselves to win."

"Yeah," said Brittany, "a balance for sure. Know when to smile and say yes and know when to offer an alternative."

"While still letting it be their choice," said Michael.

"They really don't appreciate how much we really do. Takes a certain skill for sure. We are always looking around corners," said Brittany.

"And some of us are better at that than others." Michael winked at Trish.

"Why do we do this again?" asked Trish.

"For the afterparty," laughed Michael, and they all clinked glasses and smiled.

"You going to the next tournament, Trish?" asked Michael.

"I'll have to see what the boss says," answered Trish. A movement had caught her eye in the group of people at the far end of the patio.

"Well, we are back on the LPGA tour next week, heading down to Mexico," said Brittany as she stood up. "Good luck at the next tournament."

"You too, Brittany," said Michael.

"Great to see you, Mike, maybe catch up at the next tournament," said Trish.

"Absolutely. Take care," said Michael.

Trish smiled and picked up her drink, heading toward

the far side of the patio.

PORTSMOUTH OLYMPIC HARBOUR, KINGSTON, ONTARIO, CANADA

While Trish was working her caddy cover in the golf tournament with Cole, Doc had been navigating across Lake Ontario, and Portsmouth harbour was in his sights. He was grateful for consistent winds, otherwise he would never have made it in time. He'd kept Trish aware of his progress so the team would know when he arrived. He expertly navigated his way into the marina and settled *Windy Girl* into her slip. As he was tying off lines, he heard familiar voices. Cole and the team were making their way down the ramp and onto the boat.

"How did it go?" Bill asked.

"We placed second," Trish said.

"Better than last."

"Very funny," Cole said.

"Did Miranda behave herself?" Bill asked.

"Most of the time." Trish eyed Cole. They laughed.

"Okay, let's all get below deck," said Cole. "We have a lot to discuss, and time is not on our side."

"Aye, aye, Captain," chimed 2Tall and Charlie.

"Hey, I'm the captain of *Windy Girl*," Bill said.

"Give it a rest," said Trish as she smacked his arm on the way down. Bill shrugged, knowing when he was outgunned.

They all settled into the seats around the table.

"Before we get to work, I wanted to share something that happened," said Charlie. "I didn't want to say anything on phones, even though they are secure lines." Everyone leaned forward, since Charlie was rarely the one to talk. "Something disturbing happened at dinner with Cynthia the other night."

"Okay," they all chimed together.

"She recognized a voice. The voice of the guy that blinded her."

"You're kidding," Trish said.

"Wish I was," Charlie said.

"What did you do?" Bill asked.

"Well, lots of people were taking photos, so I thought it was probably just some celebrity, but Cynthia was pretty sure. So I went over and took a short video to get his voice recorded, and I took a photo."

"Let's see," Trish said.

Charlie pulled out his phone and started scrolling through his photos.

"Jesus, Charlie, today," Bill said.

"Give me a second. Here." He turned the phone toward the group, and they all leaned in as he hit *play*.

When it was over they leaned back with sober looks on their faces.

"So, any idea who they are?"

"Yeah, I'm surprised you didn't recognize her," Cole said.

"Maybe he was more focused on the angry guy with her," Trish said.

"True," said Cole and paused for effect. "That woman is the minister of justice."

"What?" Charlie gasped.

"And that man with her is…"

"Andrej Sokol," Trish finished.

There was only the sound of water lapping against the hull of *Windy Girl.*

"Holy fuck," Charlie said.

"Shit," said 2Tall.

"Sokol was that thug all those years ago?" Charlie asked. "The guy who owns the golf course?"

"Could be a mistake, right? I mean, maybe she just thought it sounded the same," Bill said.

"I've known Cynthia a long time," said Charlie. "She is very solid. Never overreacts, not emotional. But she was rattled last night. And so was the woman Sokol was with. The guy had that same aggressive vibe."

"That woman, the minister, is his wife," Trish informed him.

That comment raised eyebrows.

"It was a long time ago, man. Nothing could stick now," 2Tall said.

"But what about the chamber in his office?" Trish asked.

"Clearly he's upped his game from the little leagues. He's not just a thug anymore," Bill put in.

"But upped it to what?" Cole said.

"I'll start doing some digging," Trish offered.

"How is Cynthia?" Bill asked.

"I convinced her to stay and finish dinner, because they left shortly after we arrived. And, well…" Charlie was blushing again.

"What is it?" Bill prompted.

"Come on, Charlie, give us the good stuff," Trish teased.

"Well, we kissed." Everyone cheered and patted Charlie on the back.

"So now you have your answer." Trish was flashing a Cheshire Cat smile. "I'm so happy for you, Charlie."

"I'm going to ask her to marry me."

Everyone brought up their hands into a big high-five.

"About fucking time," Bill said.

"Shall we break out the bubbly?" 2Tall suggested.

"Wait until the guy actually asks," Trish said.

"What could have been a disastrous evening turned into one of the best of my life. All because of Mr. Sokol."

"Well, Mr. Sokol seems to be in a rather tangled mess as far as I can see, but all roads are leading back to him.

Right now, we're two steps behind. I don't like being behind," Cole growled.

"Me either," 2Tall said.

"Talk to me," said Cole.

"Well, first, we have to get inside," 2Tall said.

"Agreed." Bill nodded.

"Glad you agree, Bill, because you're the 'in' guy," Cole said.

"When Cole and I were in that room at the golf course, we came across info about a trucking company that Sokol owns. We did a little digging around, found out some good shit, but we need to get inside that operation," Trish said.

"Yeah, because it looks like that could be a front for a lot of his dealings," Cole said.

"He has three colleagues at his side—Leonard, Misha, and Katya. Misha appears to be running this trucking company."

"And maybe they could use another driver," Bill said.

"Exactly." Trish smiled.

"But they won't just take anyone. You'd have to fit in," 2Tall added.

"Yeah, he's right," Trish said.

"Well, I did a little digging," said Cole. "Misha frequents this bar outside of Kingston. He's always looking for drivers. Must have a big turnover in that line of work."

"Why's that?" Charlie asked.

"Do we want to ask that question right now?" 2Tall said.

"Maybe not right now," Charlie said with a smirk.

"Apparently he's down one right now," Cole said.

"So he needs to see that Bill can hold his own…" 2Tall said.

"…in a fight, and when they look into him, which they will. I'm figuring they are going to hire truckers with an edge," Cole said.

"I have a buddy who will lease us a rig," 2Tall added.

"Trish, how fast can you create the persona of Bob the trucker with an edge?" Cole asked.

"I'll have it online by the morning. But if we're going to put him into a fight at the bar, who is he going to fight?" 2Tall asked.

Everyone sat, looking at the same point in space, and then they all said the same name together: "Jim."

"Set it up. Let's get Bill in the door. Then we'll work out the rest of the details later," Cole ordered.

OUTSIDE KINGSTON, ONTARIO, CANADA

Trish and Bill did their research. Misha did indeed manage a trucking company. He had a reputation of being harsh but fair, paid well, fired easily, and replaced quickly. Anyone was happy to get a job, but employees were never sure how long they would last and many never knew why they were let go. But the revolving door would work to their advantage. When they started digging into what the company was all about, that was when things got a little slippery. It wasn't anything they could actually grab on to, which was all the more reason to get someone inside. Something just didn't smell right. It hadn't since Niagara Falls. They decided Bill would become Bob Thorn. He was between jobs, owned his own rig, was happy to transport anything that would make him a buck, and wasn't one to take shit. And when Jim Morrison was approached to be part of an operation that could get the guys that messed with his daughter, well, let's just say he was overjoyed.

Bill, a.k.a. Bob Thorn, started hanging out at the local truckers' bar down the road from the golf course. He'd have some beers, play some pool, and caught the eye of the pretty waitress (always good to have a waitress on your side). Her name was Wendy: tight jeans, nicely packed blouse, brown hair pulled back into a ponytail, mid thirties, great smile, great ass. He started telling her how his rig was tired of waiting for the next job. He was loud and vocal about it. A few other guys came over to give their condolences, remembering when they were in the same boat. Bob relayed all of this to the team as they put together their next scenario.

They started getting used to seeing him. Word got out. People started calling him by name when he walked in: "Bob, any luck with a new gig?" Bob made it known he wanted work. Wanted to be hauling again. And then, one night, Misha arrived. Watched. Listened. And then he came a second night. Game on.

The next night, Bob was playing billiards, joking around with the other truckers, his beer sitting on the edge of the pool table, when Misha strolled in. He sat at the bar, ordered a beer and surveyed the room. Bob sent Trish a text letting her know everyone was in place. Trish and Jim would be walking through the door any minute. "Go and have a look at the sweet rig sitting outside, boys," said Bob, before sinking a ball in the corner pocket. "Silver grey and ready to roll."

He was waving around a pool cue with one hand, chugging his beer with the other. Misha sat and watched. The place was in high spirits. Then Jim and Trish staggered into the pub, looking slightly inebriated, and sat in a booth. Her hair was pulled back into a ponytail, and she wore snug jeans and a very tight pink sweater. She was chewing gum, popping it in her teeth and looking unhappy. The guy wore a checkered flannel shirt and a ripped pair of Levis with a big belt buckle in front, his hair was greased back. He was cussing when he walked in. Within minutes of sitting in the booth, they were arguing, getting louder and louder. Finally, the woman stood up and hollered, "You're a fucking asshole," slapped him in the face, and ran into the ladies' room.

The guy ordered another beer and moseyed over to the pool table. On his way over, he grabbed the waitress's ass, then put his hand around her wrist and pulled her toward him. Bob couldn't hear what he said, but he could see the look on the women's face; she wasn't pleased, and kept trying to push him away, but the guy held firm. It was all going like clockwork. Bob dropped his pool cue, took one step toward the guy, pulled Wendy away, and put him in a headlock. The whole bar went quiet. But before Bob could inflict more pain, the woman came out of the restroom, saw what was happening to her boyfriend, and raced over, jumped on Bob's back, screaming, "Let him go, let him go."

A couple of guys pulled the woman off, kicking and screaming. Her boyfriend then whirled around and landed a punch right on the side of Bob's head. What ensued was a barroom brawl, fists and blood and furniture flying everywhere. Finally, having had enough, Bob grabbed the boyfriend by the shirt and threw him out the door with his girlfriend not far behind. Everyone cheered, and someone started buying drinks.

Bob was a hero. He sat at the bar with an ice pack on his head and a beer to his lips. Wendy hovered and glanced his way.

The guy to his right put his beer mug down and leaned over in Bob's direction. "That was quite the shit-show."

"I like a good shit-show," said Bob, moving the ice pack around on his head.

The guy laughed and extended his hand. "Misha."

Bob put the ice-pack down and shook his hand. "Bob."

"Nice to meet you, Bob. Word is, you're looking for a job."

"Yeah, just been a bit slow as of late. You know of anything happening?"

"In fact, I do. I manage a trucking company and am down a rig and a driver right now. Interested?"

"Tell me more." He put the ice-pack back on his head.

"We move military furniture from province to province, state to state. And pharmaceuticals. Your rig equipped with a reefer?"

"What rig doesn't have refrigeration? Too much cargo requires it these days."

"This is long-haul trucking. I needed someone

yesterday. Whadda you say?"

"I say where do I sign?" Bob put the ice-pack on the bar, and Wendy came and picked it up, smiling.

"I have a shipment that has been waiting too long. Needs to head out ASAP. Can you be at the yard early to-morrow morning? Get your paperwork all done, and you can be on the road."

"I can do that."

"All right. I've lost a few drivers as of late. Hope you're in this for the long haul." He laughed at his own pun.

"I am. I like to work."

"And you can hold your own. Good to know. This business can get a little off-colour at times."

"Don't I know it."

"Here's my card. I'll see you tomorrow morning." Misha placed the card on the bar, looked Bob directly in the eye, and walked out the door.

Wendy walked over to Bob, handed him another ice-pack, and put another pint in front of him.

"Thanks."

"That one's on me," said Wendy. "Thanks for sticking up for me."

"No means no, right?."

"Well, comes with the territory it seems. Lots of jerks come in here. That guy that was just talking to you? He can be a real piece of work."

"Seemed pretty decent."

"Yeah, he can play a good game. But I've been here a while. Eventually they all show their true colours, and his can be pretty ugly."

"Good to know. Seen him in action?"

"Oh yeah. He doesn't hesitate to start a fight, and he always makes sure he finishes them, if you know what I mean."

"I do. Thanks for the heads up."

"Hey, I get off in about half an hour. Want to show me that rig outside?"

Bob put his hand up to his head and smiled. "My head feels better just thinking about it."

"See you there in thirty." Wendy winked as she went to finish up her shift.

Bob chugged the rest of his beer. He sent Trish a quick text to see if he and Jim were okay. And to let Jim know he had quite the right hook. Her text said they were nursing their bruises too, but scotch and ice on *Windy Girl* was helping. Bob smiled and sent back a few emojis. He told her he got the job, starting next day. *That's the skinny for now, I have company coming. Oh ya...don't ask for details. Let's connect at 4am tomorrow.* And he put his phone on silent.

Bob walked out of the pub and over to his rig. They were lucky that 2Tall had a buddy in the trucking business, willing to rent out this rig for a few weeks. Bill was hoping it wouldn't be any longer than that. He'd even taken Bill out and given him some driving tips. Driving a rig was an art. Bill had driven a rig in the past, but this friend of 2Tall's took it to a whole new level. Bill was having fun as well as giving more credibility to his cover. Saying yes to Wendy was now part of that cover. He smiled to himself as he walked to the rig; sometimes going undercover was hell, and sometimes it definitely had its perks. He climbed up into the berth, straightened up a few clothing items, and heard a light tapping. He opened the door slowly.

"Wendy, what a pleasant surprise." He smiled widely, opening the door and offering her his hand. She climbed in and stood beside him in the small but impressive space.

"Wow, this is gorgeous." The berth was spacious for a truck. A few van Gogh prints hung on the wood-toned walls, emerald-green curtains on the small window, the same fabric covering the cushions and comforter on the bed. A candle burned on top of the small fridge.

"Can I offer you a beverage?" Bob opened the mini fridge and grandly gestured at its contents: sodas, juice, and beer. She sat down on the bed, since it was the only piece of furniture in the bunkie.

"Beer is great. Thanks."

He pulled out two beers, twisted off the caps, and handed one to her; the other went to his lips. He took a few gulps, watching the bottle find her succulent mouth. Bob sat on the edge of the bed beside her, leaned over and pushed play on the CD player, and Eric Seckel created the mood of blues. Wendy stood up and put her beer down on the top of the fridge, taking Bill's and placing it there as well. She turned and stepped between Bob's legs, putting her hands onto his shoulders, leaning down and kissing him on the mouth with those full red lips. His hands slid up to her well-rounded ass he'd been looking at longingly for days, and it wasn't minutes before their clothes were on the floor and their limbs were wound around each other under the green cotton sheets.

She nestled onto his chest, feeling his breath coming and going, matching how breathless she felt, basking in the afterglow.

"Want to go again?" He rolled toward her and slid his tongue over her nipple, his eyes looking up for her answer. He decided it was a yes.

She leaned in, close to his ear. "Why don't you get on top this time," she said.

"You in a rush?"

She smiled, shaking her head from side to side, enjoying each moment of ecstasy, and rested her head back onto the pillow, arms behind her head. "There's a good boy. Want a little treat?"

A coy smile played with Bob's lips.

"Down, boy, there's a good boy."

Her head flopped back onto the pillow, her eyes closing. His tongue began to trace a line from between her breasts to around her navel and belly button ring and then along her hip toward her inner thigh. He paused. His eyes glanced up to meet hers. She sighed, bringing her hands forward and running them through his hair. And then she was grabbing the sheets on either side of her as his tongue found the wet warmth between her legs. It was proving to be a long-haul kind of night.

EASTERN RIDGE GOLF AND COUNTRY CLUB, KINGSTON, ONTARIO, CANADA

Misha took his coffee mug and swung his chair beside Andrej, who was busy at the computer in the secret chamber. It was getting late, and he needed the caffeine to stay awake.

"I found a driver."

"Where?"

"I've been back at the pub the last while. There was this guy that kept coming in looking for work. He got into a fight and beat the shit out of this guy. That's when I decided he'd work for us."

"Did you look into him?"

"He's a trucker. Been doing it for while. That's all I care about."

"That's all he's going to do."

"Right."

Sokol ran a tight business. He had up to eighty-five tractors and trailers on the road at any given time. The majority of work came from moving office furniture for Canadian and American armed forces, from Los Angeles to New York and across Canada. And transporting pharmaceuticals. There was always room amidst that cargo for contraband that amounted to millions of dollars in illegal profits… trafficking girls paid even more. But on the outside, it was a trucking company, plain and simple.

"Worked out the details yet?" Andrej asked.

"He'll arrive at the Eastern Transport yard first thing tomorrow."

"What does he usually carry?"

"Standard stuff, but he has a reefer on his rig, good for most of what we will want him to haul."

"Was there any problem with the last shipment?"

"Of girls or drugs?"

"Drug shipments usually go smoothly. So I'm talking about the girls."

"That was a number of months ago. Hajek was causing some noise. Wanted to get in on the deal."

"Why wasn't I made aware of this?" The temperature rose in the room.

"Because I handled it. Hajek is always looking for handouts."

"How did he know we had a shipment of girls on the way?"

"How the fuck do I know that?" Misha said. "He's fucking Hajek, he knows. He operates a huge syndicate in Niagara Falls."

"Well, he wants to meet, and I'm pretty sure I know how the conversation will go down."

"He wants in on the next shipment?"

"That's my guess, and he has an ace up his sleeve he's

likely to play. I don't trust him."

"Who does? These shipments are always a problem one way or another."

"Girls are big money but big headaches. Good we spread those shipments out."

"We spread those out because they can be high-pro-file…"

"And we keep a low profile, until Leonard went out of territory and got creative," Sokol said. "Fucking asshole. And in Hajek's territory. What was he fucking thinking. And it was one girl. What the fuck."

"Well, he knew we lost that one girl a few weeks ago. Maybe he was just spreading his wings."

"Why didn't he spread them in Toronto, or Ottawa?"

"Maybe he wanted to be out of your zone."

"Misha, he's been doing this as long as we have, he knows everyone has a zone and that you stay out of it. Period."

"Niagara Falls is a hot spot. Maybe he thought he could get away with it."

"Well, he didn't. Not by a long shot. Do we even know who grabbed the girl? Was it police?"

"No, we'd have heard something by now. Anyway, it's over. Leonard's a bit of a slow learner, but he's learned his lesson."

"Well, if he hasn't I may have to teach him a

permanent one." Misha stared at Sokol. "We've been in this a long time, Andrej."

"Yeah, and if we're going to stay alive, we can't have any more fuckups, period." He paused, letting that sink in. "I'm the boss here, Misha. Don't forget it. We're not just a street gang anymore. Keep Leonard on a short leash or I will."

Misha just sat.

"We have a new pickup arranged. This new driver will move drugs hidden in with the pharmas?"

"For the most part."

"Meaning?"

"There's that new shipment of girls coming in from Slovania. But we don't move them in the big rigs, better to use those panel vans, and I'm down a driver."

"So get him in a panel van. And figure out a way to make it happen so he stays in the dark about the operation."

"Exactly what I plan to do."

"Good to hear, Misha. Guess I'll be keeping you around a bit longer after all." Sokol smiled and patted Misha on the back as he stood to leave.

EASTERN TRANSPORT YARD, KINGSTON, ONTARIO, CANADA

Bob's tractor-trailer was so sparkling clean, you could have eaten off the cab. He wanted it shining as he pulled into the yard for the first time. He rolled to the security gate, and a guard approached the cab.

"Thorn?"

"Yup. That's me."

The guard turned away, radioing someone, then turned back and waved Bob through. As he shifted the rig into gear, he noticed that the yard was well fenced, cameras and barbed wire everywhere. There was a tighter fenced compound farther back in the yard with a number of trailers parked, their reefers running. Bob pulled up to the main building, parked, and climbed out of his rig. He took in the surroundings as he walked over to where the dispatcher was standing, talking to some other employees.

"Bob Thorn?"

Bob nodded. The other drivers nodded and walked to their rigs.

"Okay." The dispatcher flipped through the papers and extended a pen to Bob. "Sign here, and here." Bob leaned in and signed; it didn't really matter what he was signing, because it all needed to happen. "Great, you should be ready to roll. Write down your cell number here. I'll send you a text and then you'll have my contact if you need any-thing on the road. Send me a photo of your driver's license and papers for your tractor; I'll need it for our files. You'll be one of three rigs leaving within the hour. You're deliver-ing office furniture to the US Coast Guard in Portland, Maine. As it's a military load, you'll have special border crossing clearance papers. Go and hook up to trailer 47 and the guys will load you up. Have a good trip."

Bob nodded in acknowledgment and turned to leave as Misha walked by, patting him on the shoulder. "Good you're here, man. As you can see, we need every driver we can get." And he walked over to the dispatcher where they engaged in conversation.

As Bob headed to his truck, the two other drivers go-ing on the same delivery stopped to introduce themselves: Joe and Barb. Joe was a big guy, not quite as tall as Bob, but heavy from years of sitting in a truck. Barb was maybe early forties, pretty but clearly tough and able to handle herself. They were both driving Easter Transport trucks, white and red letters plastered along the side.

"Morning," said Bob, extending his hand. "Bob Thorn."

"Barb." They shook hands.

"Joe." He nodded.

"How about I just bring up the rear and follow you guys?"

"'Bout right. Barb usually leads the way. We'll swing through Montreal and then head down into the States. We're looking at about eight hours."

"Not counting the lunch stop partway down," added Barb.

"Barb never misses a meal." Joe laughed.

"Got your cell on ya?" Barb asked.

Bob pulled out his phone.

"Just in case, here's my number, and Joe's."

"See you on the road," said Joe.

Joe and Barb walked over to their rigs, and Thorn turned to watch his trailer being loaded. Out of the corner of his eye he saw a black Cadillac Escalade parked along the side of the building and a black Chevy Tahoe right beside it. He started walking around his rig, inspecting but trying to get close enough to take a photo of those vehicles and send it to Trish to do a license check. He started taking pictures of them loading his trailer, and if anyone asked he'd say it was his policy, proof for customers, but while taking those photos, he was able to get a few of the Cadillac and Chevy. He sent them directly to Trish.

Barb leaned out the window. "Let's get rolling. I'm not getting any younger here."

Bob secured his trailer, climbed into the truck, and fell in line with the two other rigs headed for Maine.

EASTERN TRANSPORT OFFICE, KINGSTON, ONTARIO, CANADA

Sokol took his seat at the head of the long rectangular steel table. Misha, Katya, and Leonard sat to his left and his two bodyguards stood behind him. Hajek, head of the crime organization based out of Niagara Falls and Sokol's biggest rival, sat opposite Sokol, his bodyguards on either side.

Over the years, Sokol had been shrewd, keeping his business separate, not invading the turf of other lords. He had amassed a solid fortune doing business his way with his small team: Katya was cunning with code books and accounting; Misha moved goods; and Leonard was the weak gopher but loyal. Hajek had called in a favour, and Sokol knew it was bad manners to say no. Years ago, when things were just getting started, Hajek had covered for Sokol, led the police off the trail and saved Sokol's ass, and he had held that favour over his head for years—until now. Sokol knew this meeting was about calling in that favour.

Sokol eyed Hajek sitting at the other end of the table, his thugs breathing heavily behind him. Sokol was having doubts, but he couldn't back out now. He regretted that the favour still hung over his head, and he wanted it gone. He hated danger lurking in corners.

"What exactly do you want, Hajek?" Sokol growled.

Hajek smiled.

Sokol's jaw clenched. "What do you want?"

"You have a shipment of girls arriving. I want half of them."

Katya glanced at Sokol. Misha eyed Katya. Leonard looked at his folded hands. They stayed silent.

"Why?" Sokol said.

"You owe me."

"How do you figure that?"

"First, you fucked up my operation in Niagara Falls."

Without turning his head, Sokol put his hand on Leonard's leg and began to squeeze. Leonard bit his lip.

"Second, I'm calling in on that favour today."

"The one from years ago? Half my shipment is not calling in that favour."

"Then messing with my turf is. Either way, you owe me half that shipment of girls."

Sokol knew he had him. But not in a million years would he let him know that. "Then we're square."

"Square."

"Then we are done. You go back to your business, I'll deal with mine…alone. Understood?"

Hajek's face reddened. He didn't like being dictated to; his hitmen tensed in response. "Stay off my turf."

Sokol nodded. "And not half the shipment. A third."

"I will not be told…"

"This is my house. This will be on my terms. One third. Final offer."

Hajek twizzled the pencil between his fingers, finally snapping it in half. Girls were hard to acquire but brought in a fortune. He was still pissed about Niagara Falls. He wanted what he was owed, he wanted this shipment. "Fine," he hissed through his teeth. "One third. As well as one third of the boxes of MDMA."

Sokol was about to ask how he knew about the boxes of ecstasy but stopped. He didn't care. He wanted this over. "And we are square."

"Square," Hajek all but whispered.

"We will divide the girls and boxes into three vans day of pickup. My vans are going to Toronto. Where do you want yours delivered?"

"I'll send you the details." Hajek stared across the table with laser focus; it was clear why he was lord in his territory. "Don't fuck me around here, Andrej."

Sokol said nothing, just maintained eye contact. "Or you me."

"You have a buyer in Toronto?"

"That has nothing to do with this deal."

"Fee upon delivery?"

"Three million now. The rest after delivery." Hajek didn't move.

"I want payment up front."

"You'll get payment at time of delivery."

"Half now, half then." Sokol's bodyguards moved to the side and drew their weapons, pointing them right at Hajek and his men.

Hajek lifted his hand up, and an envelope was passed to him. He slid it down the table. Sokol opened it. "This isn't even a fraction of half."

"Let's just say I consider your debt paid."

Sokol slammed his fist on the table, which rattled a metallic echo. He spoke quietly. "The debt is paid by me sharing my shipment, not sharing it for free. You have been saved the work of acquiring the girls and all the shit that goes into getting them here. One van of girls. The debt is paid. Three million. It's a bargain, and you know it." His bodyguards readied their weapons, and Sokol, quick as a viper, whipped a knife in Hajek's direction, finding its mark in the neck of one of Hajek's men standing behind him. He fell face-first into the table and rolled off onto the floor, blood smearing across the table's reflective metal sheen. The other hitman drew his weapon.

"Three million now, three million upon delivery," Sokol repeated.

Once again, Hajek lifted his hand, and an envelope was placed into it. Again, he sent it down the table. Sokol checked the contents. "Send me where you want your van delivered. I'll let you know when we leave the container yard. Make sure all the money is in the envelope when the van arrives. My driver will wait for payment before unlocking the contents."

"This isn't over," hissed Hajek.

"Oh, yes it is." Sokol stood and walked out of the room, Katya, Misha, and Leonard following. His bodyguards stood with weapons ready until he had left the room, then ushered Hajek and his men out of the building.

ALICE'S DINER, MAINE, U.S.A.

The drive through Ontario and Quebec had been routine, no surprises. Bob was ready to stretch his legs, he wasn't used to sitting in one place for such an extended period of time. He was relieved when he saw Barb pull into Alice's Diner, Joe right behind her, so he followed suit.

The diner had a large parking lot, obviously catering to truckers from across the country. There were rigs of all colours and sizes, license plates from across the country and from across borders. They were all neatly parked beside each other, like slices in a loaf of bread. Bob parked his rig beside a orange and blue truck, license plate Mexico. He creaked himself out of the seat and onto dry land, stretched, and looked around as he waited for Barb and Joe.

Joe caught him by surprise, giving him a slap on the back. "I get mighty stiff too," offered Joe. "Not as easy sitting in a rig when you get a bit older, that's for sure."

"What are you boys whining about?" Barb asked. "Let's go and get some food, I'm starvin'"

They made their way into the diner, which was as full as the parking lot—a melting pot of characters that had seen more country and problems than they cared to share. For a packed place, it was pretty quiet, everyone focused on their coffee, flat tires, headlights, and running boards;

standard trucker fare. It was old-fashioned and bright, lots of booths with blue vinyl seats and shiny cream tabletops with aluminum trim around the edges. The three stood at the entrance, looking for an empty table. A waitress caught their eye and waved them over to a booth. Once they were seated, another waitress, who looked like she wanted to be anywhere but where she was, came and dropped three menus on the table and proceeded to pour coffee into the white mugs already sitting in front of them. She pulled some creamers from an apron pocket and dropped them on the table. "Need a minute?" she asked.

"No, we're good," said Joe. "We'll all have the breakfast special. Couple of flat tires, two headlights and a pair of running boards." The waitress didn't write anything down, just nodded.

"Can you make my running boards crisp and I don't like my headlights runny. Thanks hon," said Barb.

"A few home fries with mine, and four flat tires for me with extra maple syrup," said Bob.

The waitress nodded again and walked away.

"We always just order the same thing," said Barb.

"Looks like everybody does," said Bob, glancing around the place. "Guess that's why she doesn't write anything down."

Everyone smiled as they hungrily embraced their coffee.

"You been working with Eastern long?" Bob asked, waving to the waitress for a refill.

"About five years now. We both started at the same time," Joe said. "You?"

"Independent. Misha sort of picked me up at a bar." He laughed. Barb smiled. Joe sipped his coffee.

"Gotta be a story there," said Barb. "Care to share any juicy details?"

"Simple really. I was in-between jobs and hanging out at this pub, playing pool and chatting up other truckers, looking for work. This asshole came in, drunk and started feeling up the waitress. She didn't like it. He didn't stop. So I made him. Turned into a barroom brawl."

"Haven't seen one of those in a while," said Joe.

"That's because you don't go anywhere after 8 p.m.," said Barb and they all laughed.

"Anyway, after the fight I was sitting with an ice pack on my head…" Barb raised an eyebrow. "Well, it wasn't a one way fight." Bob shrugged his shoulders and continued. "So as I was sipping a beer, on the house by the way, this guy came over, gave me his card, and asked if I wanted to drive."

"And here you are," said Joe.

"And here I am," said Bob. "Good place to work? I mean, I'm wondering if I want to be permanent or not."

"I mean, they pay on time, pay well, and usually the

loads are furniture or pharma. I mean, you know, I've been here five years, no need to go elsewhere," Joe said.

"Yeah, he's right. It works. But I'd like to be one of them senior drivers. You know? They seem to get better routes and are paid more," Barb said.

"Senior drivers?"

"Yeah, it's all a bit hush-hush. But ya know, drivers talk. And their truck numbers are not on our TV monitors like the rest of us."

The waitress came and put down plates piled with huge pancakes, bacon the size of the pigs they came from, and Bob's potatoes were falling off the edges. "Ketchup?" The waitress didn't wait for an answer as she reached into her apron and put the Heinz bottle on the table.

They dug into their food.

Joe looked over at Barb. "Did you hear them senior drivers are transporting small loads with panel vans now?"

"That would be a sweet job. Must be between-province runs of pharma stuff."

"Guess it's stuff that doesn't need reefers," Joe said.

"Would certainly be better on gas than these big rigs," Bob added.

"Maybe that's why they're doing it," Barb said. "Save the rigs for long-haul trips where drivers need the berths."

"Jimbo got on a senior driver's gig. Said the money is good," Joe said.

"Jimbo?" Bob asked.

"He's a driver that's been around Eastern for a while now. Good guy, bit surly," Barb said, washing a mouthful of pancake down with a swig of her coffee.

"Yeah, he's okay," said Joe. "Told me they stay at the Marlowe Motel before a road trip as some drivers come from out of town. Guess they want to make sure everyone leaves together."

"Yeah, and they don't have their trucks to sleep in. But there?" Barb asked. "Such a dive."

"Who knows? But they must need drivers, if they're bringing in outside guys," Joe said, taking a mouthful of coffee. "No one questions what the boss says. Especially when you're making money like that."

"Quick trips would be a nice change," Bob said. "How do you get in on this?"

"Not sure. Maybe it's when you've been around a while. Jimbo said he just got a call asking him if he wanted to be a senior driver."

"So old farts like us?" Barbs said. They all laughed.

"Or maybe just seasoned with the company," Bob said.

"Yeah. Maybe. But who are these outside guys? Doesn't really matter to me, I'll just drive my rig. Jimbo said they've got a gig coming up in Montreal this week. He was all happy about staying at the Marlowe. Go figure.

Maybe they have great parties there," Joe said.

"Ah crap, even if they need another driver, I'm already on the road," Barb said.

"Me too. Maybe we'll get the next one. Let's just ask about becoming a senior driver sometime," Joe said.

"Hey, Bob, see if you can get in on the gig, then you can sneak us in the door. The panel van might be a nice change, if you don't mind the flea bag." She gave him a nudge.

"Don't think I'm 'senior' enough yet," Bob said, winking.

"Well, you've got enough grey up top," said Joe, who started laughing and ribbing Bob, not seeing the coffee mug in his hand. Coffee went sailing into the air. They all laughed, grabbing napkins.

"Look into it, Bob," said Barb.

"I will do," said Bob.

"Let's finish up, boys. I'll just visit the ladies' room, then we should hit the road. I don't like to be late for a delivery."

PORTSMOUTH OLYMPIC HARBOUR, KINGSTON, ONTARIO, CANADA

Trish didn't waste a second digging into the information that Bill had sent her. And she figured it was just what Cole was hoping to find.

"Sokol was at the truck yard the other day."

"Well, he does own it," Cole said.

"But the other vehicle parked outside is registered to a numbered company."

"What other vehicle?" 2Tall asked.

"Bill sent photos of a black Escalade and Tahoe. Parked beside each other."

"Ahhh, so sweet. Even criminals have friends," Charlie put in.

"And that same numbered company is also on title for a container company at the shipping yard at Montreal's harbour," Trish said.

"Okay, more interesting," Cole said.

"He must use the truck yard as a meeting place for other thugs," 2Tall suggested.

"You think that's what was happening?" Trish asked.

"Most likely. They have to make their devious plans somewhere."

"Coincidence that the trip is to Montreal this week and that the black mystery vehicle owns a container company in the same city?" Cole asked.

"Are you thinking what I'm thinking?" Trish said.

Everyone nodded.

"So the 'senior drivers' are picking up girls in those vans," 2Tall said.

"Very likely. Not guaranteed, but likely, or they'd just use rigs for pickup. Plus, girls are usually shipped from overseas in containers. We could be wrong. Could just be more contraband. But let's prepare for the worst," Cole said. Everyone nodded.

"I checked at the Marlowe Motel. Three rooms are booked to a John Smith this Thursday," Trish said.

"Maybe they'll be a bit lonely," Charlie said.

"Poor guys. Let's provide them with some entertainment." 2Tall chuckled.

"We'll grab one of the 'senior drivers,' coax some info out of him. Plus, it means they'll be down a driver..." Cole said.

"And Bill can fill in," 2Tall finished.

"You got it," Trish said.

"Plan?" 2Tall said.

"Trish, find some revealing clothing," Cole said. Trish raised her eyebrows. "Come on, we need to get this done fast. We have to use tits and ass, yours in particular, to get what we want."

"Maybe they're into guys," she said.

"Maybe. That's why we will have 2Tall there too, in some designer jeans." Cole smiled. 2Tall wasn't smiling.

"Rather helpful that Eastern didn't cheap out and make them all share a room," Charlie said.

"Yeah, makes it easier to grab the one we need," 2Tall added.

"Best if we take the guy out the back bathroom window so no one is the wiser," Cole suggested. "We want this to all go down without a peep, attract zero attention." Everyone nodded.

"The other two won't know what happened to the guy when they get up the next morning," said Cole.

"They'll probably figure he changed his mind about the job," said Trish.

"They'll just let Misha know they need another driver," 2Tall said.

Cole nodded. "Exactly."

"Where are we going to take him for our little discussion after?" Charlie asked.

Trish laughed. "You're practically giddy, Charlie."

"Itching for a new finger?" 2Tall asked.

"Haven't had one for a very long time." Charlie smiled.

"I'll source out a farmhouse on the outskirts of town. Very secluded. We can chat with him there and then secure him in one of the upstairs rooms until it's safe to release him," Trish said.

"Good idea," said Cole. "And we'll rotate who goes to take him water and food until it's the right time for him to leave his farm holiday," Cole said. "At the Marlowe, we only need one guy. Let's stay alert, use our distractions and get the job done."

"Copy that," everyone said simultaneously.

"Charlie…" started Cole.

"Yup, I'll set up surveillance late afternoon across the road."

"Good. I can sneak around back and climb in Trish's room from the back window. When I give you the code word…"

"Which is?" Charlie asked.

"How about 'fingers.'"

"Niiice."

"When I give you the word, drive around behind the office and wait. We'll dump the guy in the back and head to the farm. Questions?"

"What's my code word so you know I'm in the room with the guy and I'm secure?" Trish asked.

"Say, 'Isn't that a small TV?'"

"Got it."

"When can I change out of my costume?" 2Tall said.

"Not until I can," said Trish, winking.

MARLOWE MOTEL, NEAR KINGSTON, ONTARIO, CANADA

Around 5:00 p.m., Charlie drove to the auto wrecking parking lot across from the Marlowe Motel. He set up surveillance. Then he waited. It wasn't until near eight that things started to happen.

"Three vans just pulled into the motel, parked outside rooms seventeen, eighteen, and nineteen. Cleary here before, since they bypassed the night clerk."

"Copy that. Keep watch. We're on our way," Cole said.

It had been a warm day leading into a sultry evening, perfect for the very short cutoffs Trish was wearing, and a tube top that was having trouble staying in place. Her hair was curled and hung loosely around her shoulders. She had her lips painted very red, long, loopy earrings, and a row of bangles jangled on her right wrist. She wore pink high heels, making her legs appear even longer.

2Tall wore a chain around his neck that dropped down to mid-chest, where his unbuttoned shirt was open. His hair was gelled up. He was wearing very tight Sergio jeans and was clearly not happy about any of it. He was told that brought an allure all its own. He hadn't laughed. 2Tall drove up in his car; about twenty minutes later, Trish arrived in hers. They parked on either side of the white vans. After checking in, 2Tall made his way to room twenty, carrying his small purple overnight bag. He walked past a 'senior driver'—tall, skinny, balding, sitting in one of the grey plastic chairs outside room seventeen. He was smoking. He made a "fag" comment, in a loud whisper, as 2Tall walked by. That's all 2Tall needed to hear. Once he entered his room, he told the team through his coms that Trish was on. There was no interest in him.

"Don't feel bad. We still love you and just love those jeans," Charlie said.

"Fuck off."

They all laughed.

"Only one guy outside, curtain's open in the other room. Two guys were lying on the beds watching TV," 2Tall said. "Falcon, once you get this guy in your room, I'll make sure you don't have other company."

"Copy that."

2Tall sauntered back out, leaning his hands on the back of one of the grey chairs, and surveyed the parking lot like it was Lake Louise. He wanted to keep watch on rooms eighteen and nineteen while pretending to enjoy the view.

It wasn't long before Trish strolled along the walkway to room sixteen, a bag slung over her shoulder, which accentuated her top. As she pulled the key out of a pocket in her bag, she dropped it, "Fuuuck," she swore and slowly bent down to get it, her breasts bulging up and almost out of her teeny top, her bag falling off her shoulder, the contents spilling onto the sidewalk.

The cigarette hung on the lower lip of the skinny guy's open, gawking mouth before it fell to the ground. She giggled and blushed, catching his eye, and made a show of pulling up her tiny shirt. She fumbled with her key while trying to collect her things, and dropped her key again. She stood up, putting her hand across her forehead. The skinny guy got up and came to her rescue. He picked up the key, presenting it to her ceremoniously.

"Oh, thank you so much," she cooed. "I seem to have butter fingers today."

"Allow me," he said, having trouble tearing his eyes away from her breasts, but he took the key and opened her door. He then bent down and picked up her bag, shoving the spilled contents inside. Falcon walked through the door, and he followed her, hoping for a reward for his gallantry.

2Tall watched. All was going calmly, quietly. The other guys were still watching TV, oblivious.

While Falcon was fumbling with her room key outside the room, Cole was sliding into it through the bathroom window.

"Thank you so much," said Falcon. "Oh my god, look at the tiny TV." Seconds split as Trish delivered one swift chop to skinny guy's throat, rendering him unconscious.

She dragged him to the bathroom. Boss heaved the body up and out the window, following behind.

"Fingers."

Charlie moved the vehicle into position. Cole hoisted the body onto his shoulder and traversed behind the buildings. Charlie had pulled alongside the motel and had got out to open the back door. Cole walked quickly, tossed the body into the back seat, hopped into the passenger seat, and Charlie headed to the farm.

"I really do hope this guy is reluctant to talk," said Charlie.

"I know, Charlie, I know."

Trish wiped down the room, collected her things, and went onto the sidewalk, gently closing the door behind her. After 2Tall heard the signal of "fingers," he wiped down his room, grabbed his purple bag, and was out front the same time as Trish. They climbed quietly into their vehicles and headed to the farm.

EASTERN TRANSPORT, KINGSTON, ONTARIO, CANADA

Bill sat in his rig. He'd driven all night, and it was the crack of dawn. Joe and Barb were probably just heading back now, having slept in their berths overnight. He'd told them he had a pressing engagement and would catch them on another haul. Trish sent Bill a text asking if it was a good time to call. From her experience, morning was always good. The answer was yes and she dialled his number. She could tell he was tired, but Bill was used to being tired when undercover. She eased him in slowly, relaying the events at the motel and how they had a driver in for questioning.

"So, was he reluctant?" asked Bill.

"Not even a little bit. Charlie was very disappointed."

"Bet he was. So?"

"So you have to drive one of those vans. This guy has worked for Misha before. And he never transports legal stuff. This time, it could be drugs or…" Trish paused.

"Or what?"

"Girls. Like we thought. They're coming in on an ocean liner. Probably from Moldova or Bulgaria would be my guess. The poverty over there is being seriously exploited in human trafficking. There are ships coming from both those countries this week."

"What the fuck do we import from Moldova?"

"Stuff like fruit juices and rubber boots and a lot of wine."

"Good wine?"

"Yeah, pretty good."

"Enough to fill a container?"

"Well, it won't be the only container on the ship, you know."

"Right. Okay. So what do you want me to do?"

"Yeah, so get Misha to let you be a 'senior driver.' We will already be at the container yard when you arrive. We'll be staked out. Waiting. So, we'll have your back if something goes down."

"Got it. What happened to the guy you took?"

"He's taking a little farm vacation."

"Meaning he can't go and blow our cover to Misha."

"Exactly. So keep doing what you're doing. We'll see you at the container yard through our scopes."

"Copy that."

Bob climbed out of his sleeper and made his way to the main building. Leonard was pacing back and forth while talking on his cell phone, he was clearly flustered. Bob stood by the coffee machine, poured a much-needed cup, and drank, listening.

"Fuck Misha, it isn't my fault." More pacing while he listened. Bob smiled as he eavesdropped on the conversation. "No one knows where he is, Misha. We only have two drivers now. Everyone else is on the road. And that shipment will be docked later today. You can't put this on me." He was yelling now. Then the call was over and he jammed his cell phone into his pocket, looking very pale. He saw Bob at the coffee machine and a slow, Grinch-style smile spread across his face.

"Morning," Leonard said, moving in Bob's direction.

"Morning," said Bob, sipping on his coffee, wishing like hell he could just crawl into bed.

"You made good time." Leonard could see that Bob was exhausted, but that was not his concern.

"I try."

"Listen, Misha has a new assignment for you. One of our senior drivers hasn't shown up for work, and we need you to make a pickup in Montreal later today. You're going to fill in."

"I'm pretty tired, man. Isn't legal for me to drive until I've had some sleep."

"But you wouldn't be driving your rig; you'll be driving a small panel van. No legalities there."

"I'm pretty tired, man."

"It's only about a three-hour drive. Listen, I could give you some blow or Provigil to keep you going."

"Where do you get that stuff? Wait, don't answer that."

"And there will be a healthy bonus when you get back."

Bob sipped on his coffee, making Leonard squirm a bit longer. He briefly considered the blow; it would certainly pop his eyes open, but he didn't want to go down that road.

"Okay, if you're that stuck, fine. But I want to be paid when I get back, not later. And cash. Under the table."

"Done. You're leaving from a motel. The vans are there waiting. Grab what you need. I'll get you a cab to take you there. All you have to do is follow the other drivers. They'll load the vans when you get there, and you just sit there, have a nap if you like, wait, and drive. Ask no questions and then follow to the delivery site. Again, all you have to do is follow. We'll make it worth your while."

"Call the cab, then. I'll just grab another coffee and something to eat." Bob turned back to the coffee machine. Leonard walked away feeling very proud of himself as he dialled Misha's number to let him know he had a driver. The vans would be at the yard on schedule. All would be ready to go when Sokol gave the word.

PORT OF MONTREAL, MONTREAL, QUEBEC, CANADA

The Wookies arrived at the Port of Montreal well before anyone from Eastern Trucking was even within sight of the water. Trish knew where the international container terminals would be. The vessel port call list she had obtained allowed the Wookies to see every ship coming into port on that particular day and from what country. That narrowed down the possible container locations quickly, which was a good thing because container terminals cover an area of approximately ninety hectares and have fifteen dockside gantry cranes with lifting capacities ranging from forty to sixty-five tonnes, yard gantry cranes and other container-handling equipment for the thousands of containers that arrive each day. Without knowing exactly where they were going, it would be like trying to find the exit in a maze of concrete and steel. And knowing the lay of the land meant there was only one place that Sokol and his vans could park to get the contents from any overseas container. That's where the Wookies would be waiting.

Once inside the gates and past security, Cole drove the F-150 to a convenient getaway spot; Trish pulled her Jeep in behind. They climbed out the vehicles, surveying the steel walls of the containers surrounding them, listening to the rumbling of the yard.

"Kind of depressing thinking of young girls travelling

across an ocean locked inside one of those," said 2Tall.

"Yeah, kind of unbelievable really," said Trish.

"If we do our job, and it does turn out that the shipment arriving today is girls, we will get them to a safe place." Cole looked at his team as they all nodded, solemnity on their faces.

"Charlie, you're very quiet. Everything okay?"

"Nothing is okay about this. I'm just trying to keep my emotions in check and focus on the job at hand."

"Good idea," said 2Tall.

"Okay, if the incoming container will be positioned around that area, then we need to be above that zone," said Cole. Everyone looked up and around the tops of the containers and other equipment in the yard. "Thoughts?"

Trish was thinking out loud. "I'll go on top of the container handling equipment over there," and she pointed to her right. "I alerted the foreman we'd be coming and may need to use some of their equipment. They've given us as long as we need and are staying out of our way." She would be prepped with Glock 19s with thirty-round mags of 9mm as well as an MP5 machine gun and binoculars, M22 7x50.

"Seeing as I'm the sniper today," said 2Tall, "I need to be belly down, so I'll get on top of that sea-can." He pointed to his left. He was outfitted with his M24 sniper rifle, chambered in 7.62 X 51 NATO and finished with a Leupold MK4 LR/T M1 10X40mm. He had always been the happiest when assigned as a sniper on a military mission. But it didn't always work as he wanted. He remembered a particular mission in the Middle East that could very well have been his last.

He had been part of a team sent to rescue the kidnapped Canadian ambassador, who was held hostage in the compound of the small village Nahrawan, just outside the city's capital of Baghdad, Iraq. 2Tall and three members of his Canadian Armed Forces Unit JTF2 were dropped off via Chinook, in the desert, just north of the village at 02:00 hours. The rebel night guards on duty outside the compound were eliminated using the stealth of blades. They had rehearsed the extraction over and over again; they knew every inch of the compound and knew exactly where the ambassador was being held. It took them minutes to secure their target. What they hadn't anticipated was missing a tripwire as they entered the building. As they moved to exit the compound, they saw they were surrounded by rebel terrorists. They sent their distress signal via satellite radio and retreated to a secure room at the rear of the compound. They knew they had enough ammunition for a very short time and would have to be patient, hoping their distress coordinates were picked up; they couldn't all get out alive with only four guys. 2Tall found his thoughts replaying his favourite movie: The Alamo. It's how he kept calm in highly stressful situations. He would have been happier at the top of the ridge with his sniper rifle. But he couldn't argue a mission. Time ticked. They heard loud voices, doors banging, feet moving. They braced themselves for the onslaught. Time seemed to hang in the thick air, slowly running like the sweat down their skin under the many layers of gear strapped to their bodies. And then, all hell broke loose: gunshots, yelling, bodies dropping to the floor, into walls. The troops sat, guns pointed at the door, trigger fingers ready. And then, a voice, a voice speaking English, Canadian English, saying their names. They held their guns in case it was a trick as the door burst open. Everyone breathed a sigh of relief as a Canadian unit stood in front of them. "Time to go boys." They all laughed, patted each other on the backs and then sobered up quickly, knowing that rebels and snipers would be waiting in the hills. They were ready. Time to get the Ambassador home.

"That rifle has an incredible scope," said Cole. Silence. "2Tall, you there?"

"Yeah, sorry. I'm here."

"You weren't playing the Alamo already were you?"

He laughed. "No, not yet."

"Okay. Let's hope you don't have to. Zone in with that superior scope."

"Why I chose it, man," said 2Tall.

"And because of that, you need to alert us to anything you see, because you'll likely see it first," said Cole. "And Charlie, you're taking the photos, which will be critical. So you need to be camouflaged and pretty close. What are you thinking?"

"I'm thinking that gantry crane looks pretty good. And it will put me at a good vantage point. Will they be needing it, Trish?

"No, you're okay," she replied.

Charlie was used to working with his Nikon DSLR camera; they had taken many unpleasant photos together at homicide scenes. And he always carried a Barrett M82A1, just in case.

"Thanks for setting all that up, Trish," said Cole. "I'll be on the sea-can opposite 2Tall, carrying my trusty McMillan TAC-50. Anything else? We ready?"

"Looks like we have the area well surrounded," said 2Tall.

"Just make sure someone has Bob's back," said Trish. "We really don't know what's going to happen here."

"Good point. We really don't. So let's watch the bad guys… and each other," said Cole.

"Copy that, Boss," they all agreed.

Now came the hardest part of the job: waiting.

As they climbed up into the respective positions, the

environment around them was rife with discordant activity. Containers were constantly being moved in and out of the yard, ship horns announced incoming vessels, sounds of traffic moving along highways echoed in the distance, a cool breeze blew off the St. Lawrence Seaway, smells of diesel gas and sitting refuse floated in the air, and seagulls circled overhead looking for scraps.

Finally, 2Tall saw the white vans and one black Cadillac Escalade approaching and alerted the rest of the team through their coms. Everyone became action-ready.

The vans and SUV drove directly to the loading and unloading dock as expected and stopped directly opposite a large, rusted container. 2Tall could see Bill in the driver's seat of one of the vans; he relayed the info. Trish peered through her binoculars, getting ready. Charlie focussed his Nikon on the spot. All the Wookies had a good view and a clear shot. They all watched as the drivers of the vans exited their vehicles, long rifles at their sides; the doors of the SUV, however, remained closed. Bob was approached by a plump man with long, stringy hair. After a brief discussion, Bob exited his vehicle, turned and walked behind the SUV, out of the direct view of the container right in front of them.

"Falcon, keep your sights on Doc," Cole said.

"Copy that."

"Tuna, keep shooting that camera," Cole added.

"Copy that." Charlie was photographing the men and

the vehicles, and then the doors to the SUV opened. Misha and Leonard walked out… but no Sokol. 2Tall directed his sights into the interior of the Escalade, but other than the driver, it was empty. "Fuck," he said. "Sokol isn't here." They all watched as Misha and Leonard walked over to the container and started to unlock the doors. Charlie zoomed in on the would-be contents. The shutter sound of his Nikon was constant, like the buzzing of a hornet's nest. As the rusty container doors opened, Charlie increased his shooting as dozens of young girls appeared, blinking and squinting in the bright daylight. They had been in darkness for days, their faces tear-streaked and dirty.

"Dozens of girls," Tuna reported to the team. "And, wait, boxes. Six sealed boxes."

"Hold all fire," said Cole. "We don't know what we're dealing with here. We don't want any girls injured."

"We need to find out where they are taking those girls," 2Tall said.

"And what's in those boxes," Falcon added.

"Where the fuck is Sokol?" Tuna asked.

"He's the king. Isn't going to show up for the dirty work," said 2Tall.

They watched as the girls were marched at gunpoint and loaded into the white vans along with the boxes. Trish counted about ten girls per van. The doors were shut and padlocked.

"I see Doc," Falcon said. "He's being directed back into the van's driver's seat by the same plump guy. Cleary they didn't want him to know what cargo he's carrying." She could see Bob look up and tap his steering wheel twice. "He's signalled. They are on the move."

"Right. Good work. They didn't make us, or there would have been a shoot out. Pack up. Get to the vehicles. We can't lose them," Cole ordered.

Trish and 2Tall swung their weapons over their shoulders, the binoculars already around Trish's neck, and raced to the Jeep. She jumped into the driver's seat and 2Tall grabbed the passenger door as she started to accelerate, pulling himself into the vehicle as the strength of inertia pressed against him. He yanked the door closed as Trish careened around a corner. "There." He pointed to the left where the vans were turning onto the highway.

Trish slowed down, keeping the vans in her sights. "Okay, we've got them," she said to Cole.

Charlie and Cole packed up their gear and headed for the F-150. "Give us your current location," Cole said. Within minutes, Cole had Trish and her Jeep in his sights. They were heading west out of Montreal toward Toronto, about a six-hour drive with no stops. They pulled onto Route 201 N out of the port, keeping a distance from the vans. After navigating traffic for about thirty minutes, Autoroute 20 W came into view. This would lead them onto the Hwy 401 West direct to Toronto.

"Those girls didn't look good getting out of that container," Charlie said.

"What were you expecting? Some don't make the trip to Toronto," Trish said in a whisper.

"Nothing we can do but follow," Cole put in.

"And hope," 2Tall said.

They drove in silence as the lines on the highway counted down the hours.

"I'm going to have to pee soon," Trish said.

"There are some roadside stops coming up between Brockville and Kingston."

"Surely they will stop somewhere," Charlie said.

"Anyone else notice those two black Tahoes that have slowly been moving up behind us?" Trish said.

"Two may be a concern," Cole said.

"They are passing now, pulling behind and alongside the vans," 2Tall said. "They're not interested in us."

"Looks like they are all pulling into that rest stop," Cole said. "'Eyes in, nose out' until I give a signal."

"You mean look but don't touch," 2Tall said.

"Yup."

"Copy that."

Cole and Trish pulled into the far corner of the car parking area, keeping an eye as the white vans and following Tahoes made their way to the back of the truckers' parking zone; the black Escalade was moving slowly toward the truckers' lot. The white vans parked. Trish had her binoculars in place. The drivers of the white vans were getting out and walking to the Escalade. Bob was out and climbing onto the roof of his van for a better vantage point. Misha and Leonard exited the Escalade. Leonard had his head down as Misha's head jutted forward, giving him orders. They turned toward the vans and seconds became hours; time collided into itself. The black Tahoes pulled alongside the Escalade, side doors slid open, and MP5 machine guns opened fire. Leonard was shot dead, along with the driver. Misha dove to the ground and Bob quickly rolled himself flat on the top of the van, away from the bullets, the Glock slipping out of his hand, falling to the ground.

Bill was in trouble. Trish, Cole, Charlie, and 2Tall came in hot, firing their Glocks as they exited their vehicles, instantly killing the driver of one black Tahoe. The other driver ran in the direction of Bob's van, firing his weapon as he ran, looking for a way out. He leapt onto the bumper of the van, vaulting himself onto the roof, away from view and bullets and coming eye-to-eye with Bob.

In an instant reaction, Bob kicked the weapon out of the guy's hand. The guy pulled a knife. Bob watched him move, waiting. To his surprise, the guy didn't start coming at him right away. He just stared, frozen. Having dropped his Glock 22, Bob was waiting to pull the Glock 27 strapped to his ankle but knew that if he reached for it at the wrong moment, he wouldn't be around to tell the story of how his day went. They were both standing now, preparing for battle. Bob expertly took the first step into the match. Before being fully settled onto his left foot, he immediately pushed back with his heel, knowing the guy would strike. He wasn't wrong. Before he was all the way back, the attacker's blade flashed into his eyes. As Bob fell to his back, from nowhere he heard Charlie yell his name. He glanced to his right as Charlie tossed his Glock 27 up to Bob; he closed his fingers around the grip. The guy lunged forward and slashed with his knife, tearing into Bob's shoulder. With adrenaline flowing, Bob didn't notice the pain of the razor-sharp blade tearing into his skin and bone and muscle, leaving a roadmap of blood on the roof of the truck. He instinctively readied the weapon in his hand and fired three rounds of 40 S&W into the guy's chest. Bob collapsed onto the roof of the van, breathing heavily.

On the ground, all hell had broken loose. Misha had started to run for a white van, but Trish was faster, knocking him to the ground. He kicked her hard, doubling her over. He pulled out his gun as Cole sped across the pavement, launching himself in the air and coming down on top of Misha. One well-placed punch and Misha was out cold. Cole dragged him over to the F-150, bound his hands with zip-ties, and threw him in the truck bed, pulling the hardtop cover closed and locking it at the side.

Bullets flew as guys from the black Tahoes started circling the vans.

"We're in the middle of a turf war," 2Tall said, almost to himself.

"We can't let them get into those vans," yelled Trish.

"Disable, but don't kill," Cole ordered. "Leave them for the cops. They must be on their way. Let's move fast."

The Wookies moved with precision and skill. Charlie disabled any occupants left in the black Tahoes while Trish and 2Tall crippled the guys trying to break the lock on the vans with shots to their knees. Cole saw a skinny senior driver racing toward the convenience store; he pulled his knife from his leg, and with pinpoint accuracy, landed it in the calf of the runaway. He fell to the ground. Cole figured another talking mouth could be helpful; he ran over to where he lay, pulled out his knife with one hand, and punched the guy in the head with the other. He wiped his knife clean and put it back in its harness. He then dragged the guy over to the truck, pulled back the cover, threw him in with Misha, and locked it back up again. Sirens were screaming down the highway; the Wookies broke open the locks on the vans, leaving the doors closed but easily accessible. They ran to the Jeep and F-150 and peeled out of the lot.

"The cops will look after the girls," said Cole through the coms. "There's enough bodies for them to figure out what happened here. Trish, fire off a secure email to the local police unit, as an alert to a trafficking crime. We were never here. We have to keep our eye on the prize: Sokol."

"On it," Trish said, as 2Tall pulled onto the 401 highway.

"Our guests in the trunk will provide our missing details later," Cole added, as he spun the vehicle onto the 401 West, in the opposite direction of the police.

"Need a few fingers for your jars, Tuna?" Bob said.

"Absolutely."

"Well, there's twenty to choose from in the truck-bed," said Cole.

"There's a first aid bag under the seat," said Charlie to Bob. "Pour some peroxide over your shoulder until we can treat that wound properly."

"Coming from the guy who keeps fingers in jars," said Bob.

"Hey, don't knock those jars. They come in handy. Plus, I know first aid. Don't want them bleeding out after I cut off the damn thing."

"Good to know," said Trish.

"Charlie?" said Bob.

"Yeah."

"Thanks man."

"Any and every time," said Charlie.

Bob put his head back against the seat. He was hoping the girls in the vans would be okay. They were all thinking the same thing.

A REST STOP NEAR BROCKVILLE, ONTARIO, CANADA

Adela sat hunched in a ball along with the other girls, leaning on the wall of the van, listening to screaming voices and gun shots going on around them outside. At least there was more light in the van and it didn't smell as bad as the container. Her nose had become used the putrid smell inside the container—smells of fear, sweat, vomit, and urine all mixed together. Each night, when most of the crew on the cargo ocean liner had gone to sleep, someone would come and march the girls around a small part of the ship while the container was hosed down. After one girl threw herself over the railing and into the sea, their walks were more supervised, and never near the edge of the vessel. While outside the container they would be given a dinner of potatoes or rice and some vegetables, occasionally some meat or fish, and drinks of water or tea. Adela always felt sleepy after drinking the tea, and couldn't remember much after that.

The girls were big ticket items; some of the men on the ship were paid handsomely to keep them alive. Breakfast was some bread and cheese inside the container. There was never lunch. They never saw the sun, only the glow of a moon when it was a cloudless night; sea breezes touched their skin as it rounded the edges of the stacked containers filled with cases of wine, cases of juice, rubber products, and other imports and items for sale. The pupils in their eyes were constantly dilated, straining to see shapes through the hard onyx dark that enveloped them inside the metal box where they lived. Adela had trouble remembering what outside even looked like, if there even was an outside anymore. She'd become a mole. A fungus. The trip across the ocean had felt like an eternity. She had marked time on the journey across the ocean by singing songs to herself, and she felt like she'd been singing for days, days of constant movement, days when she wanted to die, days that were really endless nights, but she kept singing the songs her mother used to sing; they just kept crawling into her brain. And she would feel herself smiling. Feel her fear step back, even for a moment. She had always loved listening to her mother sing, and they often would sing together when out for a walk or doing chores. She loved music. Her father taught her the dance steps for their traditional Horă and they would dance around their living room with her siblings. When she sang, he said her pretty blue eyes sparkled and her blonde hair danced a Horă. She was a pretty girl, everyone said so, tall for her age and smart to boot. She had dreamed of becoming an aeronautical engineer one day and had started to learn English to expand her school options. But money was tight after her father lost his job; her mother worked her fingers to the bone as a seamstress, but jobs were very scarce, and her brother and sister were too young to help. So it fell on Adela to leave school and help make some money as food and basic needs in Chişinău were very expensive. She learned about a company that was hiring cleaning women to work in a local factory. So she decided, reluctantly, to go for the interview, knowing that leaving school meant leaving her dreams behind as well. When she arrived for her interview, there were lots of other girls her age and some a bit older. They were all asked to fill out some forms and then were escorted to a van that would drive them to the factory, so they could see their place of work. The next thing she knew, she was locked inside the container, en route across the ocean. She was 15 years old.

When the container opened, the first thing she saw as her eyes blinked away the brilliant sunlight, her hand coming up to shied her face, were rifles. The first thing she heard were voices yelling in a language that was not her own. She recognized some words but her brain was a maze of fog and her body was weak. She had no idea where she was or where she was being herded…her eyes couldn't adjust to the light fast enough to take it all in. And before she knew it, she was pushed along with the some of the other girls into what looked like a smaller container. Doors were slammed shut, locks were clunked into place, and it was dark again, cold, and she knew they were moving, but this time the floor she was sitting on wasn't swaying from side to side, it was vibrating. Vibrating. Vibrating. She fell asleep. And then the vibrating stopped. They had stopped. And that's when the gun shots began.

EASTERN RIDGE GOLF AND COUNTRY CLUB, KINGSTON, ONTARIO, CANADA

Sokol's phone buzzed on his desk.

"Sir, you have an urgent call," his secretary told him over the intercom.

"Who is it?"

"They refused to say, sir."

"Fuck. Put him through."

"It's a she, sir."

"Then put her through."

"We have a problem," said Katya.

"What kind of problem?"

"Leonard is dead. Misha has been taken."

Sokol stood upright, items crashing to the floor from his desk. His voice was almost a whisper. "What?"

"You heard me."

"Who?"

"We were double-crossed. It was Hajek."

"MOTHERFUCKER!" And he pounded the desk with his fist, over and over again until blood started to smear across the glass. "I knew he was lying. FUCK!"

Silence.

"Goddam fucking Leonard," said Sokol, almost to himself. "All these years, all this work, and one stupid mistake puts us all at risk. Why did no one know what he was planning in Niagara Falls? Because now, this is war. We have no choice. Hajek will keep coming. We have to stop him. Square my fucking ass. A square shot to his head is what he needs. Where were you?"

"Where the fuck do you think I was? In uniform as Officer Stokely, coming to rescue the fucking girls that were supposed to be our meal ticket for the next while."

"You couldn't do anything?"

"Like what, drive away with the girls? I had to rescue them, for fuck's sake."

"Then we have to make our next move. Was this all because of Hajek?"

"Absolutely. It was all going as planned before his Tahoes and his thugs showed up. But then, these guys who started shooting at everyone, I can only think that it must have been some undercover group that got a tip."

"Wouldn't you have heard about that?"

"Not necessarily. Undercover ops stay pretty quiet. Could it have been another gang?"

"Not likely. We would have known about that."

"So somebody's been leaking info. Just a matter of time before I find out who and to whom. But if those undercover guys hadn't shown up, it would have still been a shit show, and that would have been all Hajek. He wanted those girls. He wanted a war."

"Then he will have his war."

"Then we need cash," said Katya. "And lots of it. Because Hajek is equipped and dangerous."

"So am I," Sokol growled. "Start making arrangements. I'll get the money we need. Son of a bitch thinks he can ambush my men, my job, my take, just like that?"

"It will take some time to liquidate and get that kind of money."

"No it won't."

"What are you talking about?"

"My safety deposit box. I'll just have to withdraw earlier than planned."

"Natalie?"

"Natalie." There was a silence. "We need to know Hajek's next move."

"I'll look into it."

"You'll look into it? What the fuck does that mean?"

"It means I'll see what I can find out." She paused. "What about Misha?"

"He's of more value to us alive than dead."

There was a long silence, like all the air had suddenly gone out of the room.

"Andrej, he'll talk."

"I know he will. That's why you have to get him out of there."

"And Leonard?"

"Always was an asshole. A liability. Good riddance."

"Fine. I'll deal with Misha."

"And how will you do that?"

"I'll figure something out. I always do."

"Yes, you do." Sokol hung up the phone and buzzed his secretary. "Get my wife on the line." Sokol started to pace around his office. He could barely contain his fury. If Hajek wanted a war, a war he would get. He was gas-fire red with fury. A fury he remembered seeing in his own father, a fury triggered by war. His mind pulled up a memory from years ago…

There was one candle sitting in the centre of the cake, a small number ten carved into the wax. Candles were hard to come by and so were ingredients for a cake, even though the second world war had ended five years ago. But Andrej's mother wanted to have a grand birthday celebration for her boy. Their neighbourhood of Nusle, in Prague, was picking up the pieces from the bombings during the war, and citizens were still dealing with rations. With the help of her friends, Andrej's mother had pulled together enough flour, sugar, cream, and honey to make a medovnik cake worth feasting on. And there was one small present, wrapped in newsprint and tied with a shoelace sitting on the table beside the cake. Andrej's two sisters and brother, older than him, as well as aunts and uncles, had all gathered in the tiny kitchen; after such sadness for so long, they relished each and every celebration. The only member missing was Andrej's father. He had never truly recovered from being captured by the Nazis. He had been part of a resistance group held responsible for killing an SS leader. In many ways he didn't believe the war was over, and his anger would rise and fall for what appeared to be tiny things to everyone else. But to him, they were subversive, and bound to be caught by the enemy. With Mr. Sokol, it was like living on the edge of a storm waiting to break each and every day. He was an intelligent man who managed a factory, as industrialization came to Czecho-slovakia early. He loved and valued his family and they returned that affection to him. He purchased large tracts of land where he hoped he would build his own factory one day, and a big house in the country for his family. He was planning on entering politics and running for office and then the war began and life changed for everyone. The land he had purchased was taken by the Nazis. He watched oppression begin and he joined the resistance movement only to be falsely accused and captured himself. The tortures he had endured at the hands of the robotic and cruel Nazis scarred him deeply. He came back a shell of the man he had once been. He now believed the demons in his head; demons placed there by the Nazis. His wrath had no measure; something his family had never seen be-fore. Andrej came to fear him… and idolize him.

As the festivities of the birthday were beginning and the family's voices were raised in song, Andrej's father burst through the door. He demanded to know why they were all making such a noise. They were sure to be heard; it would attract SS attention. In one fell swoop, all the carefully placed pieces on the table were crashed onto the floor, the gift sliding under the kitchen cabinet, hidden from view. Andrej's mother was crouching on the floor, her tears mingling with the cake she had so lovingly made as she desperately tried to pull it back together from the floor and onto the plate, not wanting to waste a scrap. Mr. Sokol's brothers took him by the shoulders, leading him out of the room, where they could try to calm him before more violence ensued, as it so often did. The children helped to clean things up and reset the table. Andrej stood silently in a corner, watching. He was 10 years old now, no longer a boy. He knew it was now up to him. He'd learned from his father to trust no one. Everything could be taken away in a heartbeat, so be cunning, clever, and beat those motherfuckers.

The phone on his desk rang.

"What?"

"Your wife is on the line, sir," Marsha said.

Andrej picked up the receiver as if picking up a weapon. "Natalie?"

"What do you want, Andrej?"

"I need one of those envelopes from the safe deposit box."

"I'm in the middle of meetings. I can't do it today."

"Yes, you can. And you will. I will meet you at the meeting spot in three hours. I strongly suggest you be there, on time."

"Andrej, I just can't be t—" But the line had gone dead.

PARLIAMENT BUILDINGS, OTTAWA, ONTARIO, CANADA

Natalie felt that familiar knot in her stomach, one that always presented itself if it meant having to go against Andrej. She often walked away with a cracked cheekbone, or a bruised shoulder, or a black eye. But why did he want an envelope now, and why the rush? He had always given her sufficient warning, sufficient time. Never this intensity. He was angry. Angrier than usual. She could hear it in his voice. Something was wrong, but she couldn't and wouldn't ever ask. He wouldn't tell her anyway. But if he was this angry, best to just cut her losses, as she was getting used to doing, and get the envelope without question.

She left the meeting room and told her secretary that she would be back later in the day. Family emergency. Not really a lie. The knot in her stomach tightened as she made her way down the sidewalk to the Canadian Imperial Bank of Commerce. It was good to get some air, and the walk helped calm her down.

She entered the bank, went through their security procedures, and then found herself alone in the vault with a large table and chairs in the middle of the room. She opened the safe deposit box and pulled out one of the envelopes. She had never opened one of these envelopes. Not once. Not in the twenty years he had been asking. It was the agreement they had made. He paid for her education and funded her campaign; she handled the safe deposit box. She had never once questioned him or looked in the envelopes he gave her. But for some reason, today was different. She wasn't quite sure why, but she knew that today she was going to look. What documents could he possibly be hiding here? They were sealed with the old-fashioned blue wax seal of his family's crest: a lion in the centre with a scorpion curled around the outside. She would say the seal cracked when she bent the envelope by mistake, taking it out of the slot. She brought the envelope with her and sat at the table, sweat beginning to form around her temples and down her spine. Her heart rate was elevated. If he knew she was doing this… she didn't let herself finish the thought.

She slowly cracked the seal, pulled back the fold of paper, and peered inside. Cash. She sat back. They weren't documents at all. There must be millions of dollars in those envelopes, she thought. She peered inside the envelope and saw a paper sitting on top of the packaged bills. She slid it out carefully. It was some kind of tally sheet, a code sheet of sorts. She had no idea what it all meant, but there were dates, colours, and words in the margin: drugs, girls, source, buyer, seller. She pulled out her phone and took a photo. She felt like she wanted to vomit. She was scared. She didn't know what it all meant, but she knew it wasn't good.

Meticulously, she repacked the envelope, making sure the sheets of paper were carefully sitting above and below the bills, that's why it always felt like documents. She pressed the wax of the seal back together as best she could, hoping the warm sweat from her hands would soften the wax enough for it to adhere together even a little bit. She put the envelope in her briefcase, walked out of the bank, and started toward the coffee shop where they always met. She saw him standing outside, leaning against the wall. She swallowed hard and pasted a smile on her face. If she kept talking while handing him the package, he might not notice the seal was broken until she was well gone. People were coming and going. It was a busy place. She was grateful for that. He saw her and started walking toward her. No words were exchanged. She kept the pasted smile on her face while reaching into her briefcase; she pulled out the file and handed it to him, seal down. He snatched it out of her hands, turned, and strode in the opposite direction. She exhaled and walked into the coffee shop, needing a moment to sit, adrenaline coursing through her veins.

She and Miranda were both in danger, that much was clear. She had to warn her daughter, but she had to be careful. She had to be absolutely sure Miranda knew nothing about these envelopes. She was going to text her, but hesitated. How could she be sure her phone wasn't bugged? Even a call could be dangerous. She would set up a meeting. She punched Miranda's numbers into her phone, hoping she'd answer; she wouldn't leave a message.

"Hi, Mom."

"Hi, honey. Your flight isn't until tomorrow, right?"

"Right. I wanted to get down there a bit early for the next tournament."

"Great. I'm so overwhelmed with meetings here, I wasn't sure if you were still there tonight. It's been such a great week. Love it when we can have time together like this."

"Yeah, me too."

"Okay, so I've pushed back some meetings so we can have a nice dinner tonight."

"Okay. but I'm at the practice range in Kingston now."

"Perfect. Let's meet at my condo at eight tonight."

"You sure, Mom? Not too much for you?"

"Nope, all good. I have a surprise planned."

"Cool. Okay. See you tonight. Love you."

"Love you too."

Natalie breathed a sigh of relief. She hoped if anyone else was listening, no red flags had gone up. Time was not on her side. She had to leave for Kingston immediately.

PORTSMOUTH OLYMPIC HARBOUR, KINGSTON, ONTARIO, CANADA

"Guess that undercover job's over." Charlie gave Bill a sideways glance.

"Well, at least my cover is still intact."

"That's true, it actually is," said 2Tall.

"I really did like that rig," Bill said.

"Nah, you just liked the girl in the sleeper," said Charlie with a wink.

"It was a nice sleeper." They all laughed.

"How's Misha doing?" Trish asked.

"Tied up in one of the upstairs bedrooms where we left him. The skinny van driver is in the room down the hall. Misha is not as helpful as the other guy. He doesn't seem to want to eat or drink either, but the skinny guy hasn't missed a meal," Cole said.

"Maybe he likes the accommodations."

"Maybe."

"Did you give Misha a bit of incentive?" Bill asked.

Charlie held up the jar with Misha's middle finger inside, swimming around in the formaldehyde.

"Incentive it is," Bill said. "So what are we gonna do with the guy if he's useless?"

"Well, he may be proving useless now but certainly dangerous if he gets out. And we can't hand him over to the police yet," 2Tall advised. "They will just have to stay put until we…"

"…until we get Sokol and this Katya. She's the only one left," Trish said.

"Yeah. I forgot about her," said Bill. "We have to get something on Sokol. We have nothing. Nothing that will stick. Nothing that connects him to Jim's daughter, the girls in those vans, nothing. He's clever and slippery."

Charlie sat, his jaw clenching and unclenching, not trusting himself to speak.

"What about those girls in the vans? Do we know what happened to them? They sure didn't look good," said 2Tall.

"Cops got 'em. They're safe," Trish said.

"Any links back to us?" Cole asked.

"No. Police are just looking into the plates on all the vans, the Tahoes and Escalade."

"Good. Gives us some time," said Cole. "They won't find anything. Those vehicle will be registered to ghosts."

"Yeah," whispered Charlie. "Ghosts."

"I'm ordering some food," said Bill. "I'm starving."

"It's 10:00 p.m." Trish shook her head.

"So, I'm still hungry."

"I'll go in on that," 2Tall said.

"Me too," Charlie put in.

"Make that three," Cole added.

"Fine. We'll order food. But what are we going to do about Sokol? Do we still need Bill undercover?" Trish asked.

"That's a good point." Cole pondered it. "Maybe we do. I mean, we are a bit stalled right now."

"We could have another go at Misha. I mean, I really just got started," Charlie said, a bit too enthusiastically.

"I know you want him, Charlie," Bill said.

"We all do," Cole said.

Trish's cell phone rang, the phone she had used when working as Cole's caddy. They all looked at each other. She looked quizzically at her phone, not recognizing the number, and picked it up. "Hello?"

"Trish?"

"Yes."

"It's Miranda."

"Miranda? From the tournament?" Trish lifted her eyebrows in an exaggerated way and looked at the guys.

"Yeah, listen, I need to talk with Cole. I don't know who else to go to."

"How did you get my number?"

"You're Cole's caddy. I have everyone's number. Anyway, I need some advice. I was hoping Cole could help. Can you give me his number?"

"Well, I can't just give out his number."

"It's important, Trish. It's about my dad. I don't know what to do. Cole is the only one I can trust."

"Your dad? Okay. I'm not sure Cole will be very helpful with a domestic matter, but here you go. I've sent you a text with his number." She looked over to Cole, who was nodding his head up and down.

"Thanks, Trish. I owe you."

"Good luck."

The line went dead. Everyone looked at each other in silence. Cole's second phone began to ring, his golf phone. He answered and put it on speaker.

"Hello?"

"Cole?"

"Yes."

"This is Miranda." She started to cry.

Another voice came on the line. "Cole, this is Natalie, Miranda's mother. I'm not sure how to talk about this. Is it possible for us to meet tonight?"

"What's this about?"

"My husband."

They all looked at each other.

"Where are you?"

"At my condo in Kingston."

"Can we talk on the phone?"

"No. This needs to be in person."

"Why exactly are you calling me? I'm a golfer, not a therapist. I'm sure there are better people you could call."

"It's not like that. Miranda told me your dad was a

prosecutor or something like that. I hoped you may have some ideas for us, or could at least point us in the right direction, maybe a person we could contact. We can't go to anyone else we know right now. Plus, she trusts you. So we are calling for help."

"Give me the address. Trish and I will be right over."

Cole hung up and looked at his team.

"Looks like we may have our hook to hang Sokol," said 2Tall.

"Let's not get ahead of ourselves," said Cole.

"He's right," said Trish. "Miranda is rather—how can I put this delicately?—she's a bit emotional."

"Well, let's hope it's something juicy that we can use," said 2Tall. "We need this."

"Wear the coms, that way we can back you up if needed," said Bill.

"Copy that," said Cole.

"We've got to get this bastard," said Charlie.

"We will," said Trish. "We will."

NATALIE'S CONDO, KINGSTON, ONTARIO, CANADA

Trish and Cole walked into the lobby of Castle High Condos. A panel of buttons opposite the locked glass doors had residents below each buzzer. Trish pushed the button with Natalie Sokol's name. "Bit weird that she has her own condo here and in Ottawa."

"Why?" Cole asked.

"Well, doesn't Sokol have a house in Kingston?"

"Maybe she needs her space, I don't know." He shrugged.

Trish thought a moment and then shrugged as well.

They waited as the ringing alerted Natalie. "Hello?" Natalie answered hesitantly.

"It's Trish."

A buzzer sounded as the glass doors unlocked. They walked over to the security desk.

"We're here to see Natalie Sokol. She's expecting us," Cole said.

The guard called Natalie to confirm. "Suite 419. Elevators are to your right, down the hall."

Trish and Cole made their way to the elevator, stepped inside, and pushed number 4. They rode in silence, each within their own thoughts. As the doors opened, Cole said, "I'm only a golf pro."

"And I'm only a caddy."

They nodded to each other, walked down the hall, and knocked on Suite 419. The door opened a crack, and Cole saw Miranda's eyes as they peered above the chain, holding the door steady. She pushed the door closed, slid off the chain, and opened the door. It was obvious she'd been crying. Once they were both inside, she quickly closed and locked the door, sliding the chain back into place.

"Thank you so much for coming," said Natalie as she walked over and extended her hand toward Cole, then Trish. "Please." She gestured toward the couch. Everyone sat down. It was not a comfortable energy in the room.

"Would anyone like anything to drink?" Natalie asked. Everyone shook their heads.

"I'm not exactly sure why you called us and not the police," said Cole.

"Fair question. As I am not entirely sure of what I am dealing with, and as I work in the government, I am hoping to have some things checked out before proceeding further. I remember Miranda saying that you had told her about your father, a lawyer, so I thought you may have some contacts we could use. And, well, Miranda trusts you. This is potentially a sensitive issue."

"What is a sensitive issue?" asked Trish.

"I'm not sure if my husband is involved in some, how shall I say it, some shady business."

"Why do you say that?

Miranda and her mother exchanged a concerned stare. Miranda nodded to her mother to continue. She took a deep breath. "My husband appears to have a large sum of money, I mean very large, secured in a safe deposit box, and I am the only one with access. It's a long story and one I'm not proud of. I never looked at what was in the envelopes before today because he made it abundantly clear, that if I was to do so, I would regret it. But today, when he told me to bring him an envelope, something was different. I could feel it. So I broke the seal on the envelope and looked inside." Everyone was listening. Natalie took a breath. "I found a strange paper inside the envelope, with all the bills."

"Do you have that?" asked Cole.

"No, but I took a photo." She swiped on her phone until the photo appeared. She handed the phone to Cole.

"This is a rather, hmmm, uncomfortable list."

"Yes, it is. That is why I called you."

"Would you mind if I took a photo of this? To show to someone I have in mind to help you?"

"Of course." Cole took out his phone and snapped a shot. He handed the phone back to Natalie.

"Give me one minute to make a call," he said as he stood and walked to the far side of the extremely large living room, out of earshot, glancing at Trish as he stepped away. Trish took the cue and started to talk loudly and with concern to Miranda and Natalie. "Oh my god, this must be so terrifying for you both. I can only imagine…" she began as Miranda started to cry and talk at the same time.

In the far corner of the room, Cole connected with Charlie, Bill, and 2Tall. "I don't have long. Charlie, book a suite at the Strata Hotel in Kingston immediately. Text me the room number. You will be staying there until further notice, with Natalie and Miranda, as protection. Get over there now. 2Tall, Bill, head over to the golf course. We'll meet you there."

"We're on our way."

Cole walked back over to the couch. The conversation stopped as they all looked up at him.

"I talked to a friend of my dad's in Homicide. He doesn't think you are safe here. So I'm taking you to a hotel where you will stay until contacted. You'll be protected there. An agent will meet you there. You are not to contact anyone at all. If we need you, we will reach out through the man who will be staying with you. Apparently his code name is Tuna. Your phones need to be turned off and stay that way."

"Can we pack a few things?"

"Very quickly," said Cole. Natalie stood, pulling up Miranda.

"I'll help Miranda," said Trish. They began to walk to the bedrooms.

"Natalie," Cole said. She stopped and turned around to look at him. "My dad's friend wanted me to ask you, do you ever remember your husband using the name Shadow Man?"

BROCKVILLE GENERAL HOSPITAL, BROCKVILLE, ONTARIO, CANADA

When the police had arrived earlier at the rest stop after receiving multiple calls about gunshots being heard, the first thing they saw were bullet holes in bodies and vehicles. They had received a tip about the contents of the white vans and so proceeded with caution. Once they opened the back doors to those vans, the scene and the stench was overwhelming; one officer had turned to vomit. The girls were all cowered into the back corner of the van when light trickled in, eyes wide with fear. A female officer, talking quietly, entered each van. It was quickly apparent that the girls spoke no English, except for one small girl who identified herself as Adela. She timidly relayed the officers' message to the other girls, that they were there to help.

The girls were clearly traumatized and drugged. Bruises were noticed on many arms through torn fabric and on tear-streaked, dirt-smeared faces. Ambulances were called to transport the girls to the nearest hospital for observation. They were dehydrated and malnourished.

Now, thirty young girls waited in a large private room at Brockville General Hospital, some in chairs, some on the floor. Ten of them were deemed as being in critical condition and were placed in an ICU ward. The others were waiting to be assessed and then moved to a secure facility. A police officer stood in the hall just outside the room. They were taking no chances. They didn't want a bad situation getting worse.

SOKOL RESIDENCE, KINGSTON, ONTARIO, CANADA

Sokol was pacing back and forth, vibrating with fury. Katya had never seen him like this. He was always calm, cool, in charge, in control. He was none of those things as she watched him now. He was afraid. Which made her afraid.

"Misha was a greedy little prick. Always was. That whole fuck-up in Niagara with that girl was Misha's doing."

"That was Leonard, you know that."

"No, it was Misha. Leonard never could have come up with something like that himself. He just wanted to take credit, thinking it was a good thing. It was the first disaster in this string of disasters. He wanted to take over that turf, and it started with one girl. That's how it always starts. He wanted to start something of his own, cut me out."

"You think Leonard and Misha really wanted to start a new operation?"

"THERE IS ONLY BUSINESS!" His face was inches from hers.

"Good. Then you'll be happy to know I took care of some."

He sat down on the edge of the couch. "What?"

"Well I found where they were holding Misha, they also had one of the van drivers. I shot him," said Katya.

"And Misha?"

The door opened and a haggard looking Misha stepped inside. Sokol stood up, marched across the room, and punched him hard in the face. Misha didn't make a move or utter a sound.

"Be glad you're not dead," said Sokol. "You'll be told what you can do to redeem yourself very soon. For now, get some food and rest. I don't want to see you right now."

Misha glanced at Katya, and left the room.

"Okay, well at least one thing went well," said Sokol. "Now, what about Natalie?"

"What *about* Natalie?"

"Maybe you should put her on your business list too?"

"Why?"

"Because she broke the seal on the envelope."

"Fuck," said Katya. "So she saw the code sheet."

"I'm guessing she did, I don't know for sure."

"But even if she did," Katya said, "what does she know?"

"Nothing. The code will mean nothing to her."

"Natalie is a national figure. I'm not sure killing her at this point is a smart move."

"But if she figures it out…" Sokol was filling with rage.

"A sheet that links to the code book. And enough words to get her thinking." It was Katya's turn to sit down.

"But it means nothing without the code book, right? There are no names on that sheet or in that book to connect us with any of those deals."

Andrej moved his head from side to side. "We have to get that code book."

"We have to destroy that book."

"Okay. I'm going to the club to get it now."

"It's 1:00 a.m. Leave it until the morning."

"I'm going now. You are going to order the hit on Hajek. There's enough money to hire the best."

"He'll be well protected."

"So hire enough guys to unprotect him." Andrej turned, grabbed his keys off the table, and stormed out the door.

EASTERN RIDGE GOLF AND COUNTRY CLUB, KINGSTON, ONTARIO, CANADA

After leaving Natalie's condo, Cole and Trish wasted no time driving to the golf club, contacting Bill and 2Tall on the way, and telling them they would be needing eyes. En route, Trish disabled the security system at the golf course. There had to be a code book that explained the sheet Natalie had photographed, and if it was going to be anywhere, it would be in that secret chamber. Cole was pretty sure that Sokol was on his way to get the same code book. It was the only piece of evidence that would implicate him. Question was, would they beat him to it?

Cole and Trish parked the Jeep off the first green. Its black body disappeared into the night. They put on their gloves and slid their backpacks in place containing equipment they might need. They moved low and quickly across the fairway toward the clubhouse. It was after midnight. 2Tall and Bill let them know they were in place and had eyes on the front and back of the building. Trish and Cole didn't waste any time getting into the chamber.

Once inside, they each started from the opposite side of the room, searching every inch with their small flashlights.

"Found something," Trish called.

Cole came over and stood beside her. There was a

hidden drawer under the counter, well back from the edge. It was locked. Cole pulled his tools out of his pack and gently coaxed it open, not wanting to leave any marks. Trish pulled out a small book. It was full of dates and names and all the codes they would need. She moved to put it in her pack.

"No," Cole whispered. "We can't take it. If Sokol sees that it is gone, we have lost our edge. He can't know anyone is on to him, or we will never get him, and we are so close."

Trish nodded and pulled out her trusty Minox EX camera, shiny lightweight aluminum, long and slim, efficient, about the size of an index finger. She started snapping photos as Cole kept turning pages. They had a few left when Cole heard Bill in his ear. "Someone's coming in hot. It's Sokol. Get out of there, now."

Cole secured the book back into the drawer, making sure it was locked. They exited and secured the chamber, left the office as it was when they arrived, and raced down the hall and out the back door. Once outside, Trish sat down quickly and reengaged the security system. They ran for the Jeep.

PORTSMOUTH HARBOUR, KINGSTON, ONTARIO, CANADA

It was 3:00 a.m.

Trish, Cole, 2Tall, and Bill sat around the table below deck.

"What now?" Bill asked.

"The code book has every transaction over the last twenty years," Cole said.

"But his name is nowhere. None of their names are. There are names, but not the ones we need."

"Fingerprints?" 2Tall asked.

"Wouldn't matter, won't hold up in court," Trish said.

"We need more," Cole said.

"Remember you told me you asked Natalie if she'd ever heard Sokol use the name Shadow Man?" Trish said.

"Yeah."

"We never finished that conversation. What did she say?"

"She said that after Sokol's dad died, he was talking about him, which he rarely did apparently. She said his dad was part of the Resistance movement against the Nazis in World War II. Guess what his handle was?" Cole said.

"Shadow Man," Bill said.

"Right. And he always told him that in order to get things done, you have to be a Shadow Man," said Cole.

"If Sokol is Shadow Man, he's running one of the most successful crime rings in the country," 2Tall mused. "Shadow Man is the elusive guy police have been searching for, for years. Even I've heard of his name. They've got his mark on so many illegal jobs, but never with a face. Never a conviction. Shadow Man and Sokol were never put together as the same person."

"Until now."

"And his golf course is his cover," Cole said. "And his politician wife. Clever."

"And Natalie is the only one who knows his secrets," Bill added.

"And she is the only one who can get him to admit he is Shadow Man," 2Tall said. "Because otherwise, it is all a moot point."

"So then we have to convince her to go and talk with Sokol wearing a wire," Trish suggested.

"That's dangerous, Trish," Bill said.

"But letting him go is dangerous too," said 2Tall. "Because Natalie having that cheat sheet makes her a target."

"Show her pictures of the girls he brings in for sex work," said Trish. "My contact told me they have all the girls at Brockville hospital and that the photos are horrific. Looks like we got them out just in time. Otherwise, we may never have found them. Maybe that'll convince her. Tell her what happened to Jim's daughter."

"And make sure Miranda is there when you have the discussion," Bill put in. "And I think Jones needs to be there too."

"Who?" 2Tall asked.

"The undercover cop that used to work with Bill. He kept the police out of the picture when we brought Hailey into the hospital," said Cole.

"Detective Sergeant Jones. We've always had each other's backs," said Bill. "Glad to see that hasn't changed. But he needs to be in on this."

"Bill's right. If this is going to stick, and goddamnit, it needs to stick, we can't miss this opportunity. We only get one shot at this. And it has to be done with the stamp of the police," Trish said.

"Okay then. I'll bring Jones up to speed," Bill said.

"He'll tell Natalie and Miranda how it all works, he'll secure the body pack, and he'll be on surveillance," Trish said.

"Exactly. That way, everything is legal on our end, and Sokol can't slither his way out," said Cole.

"Do we tell Charlie?" Trish asked.

"Not just yet. He's too close. Too angry."

"Hey, Cole." Cole looked in Trish's direction. "Remember how Charlie said way back when Cynthia was hurt, how they tried to drag her into their van?"

"Yeah."

"Do you think he was going to use her for the sex trade?"

Everyone eyed each other, not daring to answer.

"Well, fuck, I do now," Cole said. "Which means, he's been doing this a fucking long time."

"We have to get this guy," said 2Tall. "We have to move on this quickly."

"Agreed. We have to set the meeting up with Natalie tomorrow morning," Trish said.

"And she'll need to set up a meeting with Sokol for tomorrow night," Cole added.

"You can be sure he's ordered a hit on whoever double-crossed him. So things stand to get very messy very quickly," Bill said.

"And people could start to disappear," Trish said.

"What about Jim?" 2Tall asked.

"No. He can't be part of this. He can't even know until it's over. Too risky," Cole said.

"He got his punches in at the bar," Bill said. They laughed.

"Speaking of punches, what about Misha?" Trish asked.

"I think he's Jones' responsibility now. Cole?" Bill said.

"Yeah, agreed."

"What if he mentions the finger Charlie has?" 2Tall asked.

"No proof. He can say what he wants. He's a thug. We have photos of him at the scene of a sex trafficking crime. He's done," Cole said firmly.

"I'll give Jones Misha's location and everything else we know to this point. He has to be in all the way now," Bill suggested.

"Okay. We have a lot of work to do before Sokol starts putting the pieces together and gets to Natalie and Miranda before we do," Cole concluded.

STRATA HOTEL, KINGSTON, ONTARIO, CANADA

Bill arranged for Jones to meet with Natalie and Miranda at 8:00 a.m., along with 2Tall, Trish, and Cole. He told him everything they knew. They all met outside the hotel, and because they didn't want to draw any attention to themselves, they introduced each other while walking into the lobby and stepping into the elevator. As it was early hours, they had the lift to themselves. Only then did they relax and begin to talk.

"Jones, I want you to take the lead in there," Cole said.

"That was my intention."

"No, I mean completely. As far as they are concerned, I am a golf pro, and Trish is my caddy."

Jones turned and looked at Cole, then Trish. "Good to know. I'll keep your cover intact. Means you can't say a thing or even react."

"Copy that. And 2Tall is also a detective today, named Hank. Hank Smith, if they ask. He works with you, Jones, okay?"

"Yeah, got it."

"I want to get this guy."

"We do too, Cole. Trust me. I have a vested interest in Shadow Man. He's been on my radar for years." Jones remembered back to when he was introduced to Shadow

Man, by default. It had all left a bitter taste he could not get out of his mouth. Just the mention of the name took him back years…

After several years on surveillance with Bill and a team of police officers, Jones was promoted to detective sergeant, assigned to the Toronto Fraud Squad and placed in charge of a special squad looking into financial money laundering. His team was referred to as the Anti-Rackets Team.

Jones and his team had a line on a high roller who was known to move large amounts of money for his select group of clients. The suspect, Warren Abrams, was smart, well educated, with an MBA, and was a chartered accountant. A big player. He worked mostly from his condos in Toronto and the Caymans. Warren was quietly sought after as a money fixer, a private man with lots of secrets, and for the past ten years he had been managing and sanitizing millions of dollars for Shadow Man's organization, as well as several other criminal organizations. He made millions.

Jones and his squad had picked up on Abrams by accident while tracking another offshore fraud gang. That's how he stepped into the world of Shadow Man, by complete accident. Through info obtained by an approved wiretap, Jones found out that Shadow Man would fly to the Caymans once a month and meet with Abrams. Jones had enough evidence to warrant a trip to the Caymans at the same time as Shadow Man would be there. But no one knew who Shadow Man actually was and intel kept coming up empty. This guy had insulated himself well.

Jones linked up with Interpol and the RCMP on the island and started poking around when he saw Abrams jumping into a cab. Jones hailed his own cab and followed, watching as Abram entered the Hilton Hotel. Jones followed and took a seat at the bar where he could easily see Abrams. After a few brief moments, a man walked up to his table. The only thing that Jones heard was the name he called him: Shadow Man. Abrams' face visibly paled as Shadow Man sat down opposite him. Jones could see the Shadow Man held a gun under table, pointed at Abrams, but he couldn't see Shadow Man's face. Abrams didn't wait, he bolted for the door, hoping the gun wouldn't be fired in such a crowed room. Shadow Man ran after him, hot on his heels, Jones not far behind.

Abrams bolted down a hall, closed room doors on either side. Shadow Man had a clear shot, fired, and hit him in the right leg. Abrams fell. Jones came around the corner just as Shadow Man moved to stand over Abrams; he watched him shoot an unarmed, injured man in the head at very close range, close enough that Abrams would have smelled the moisturizer Shadow Man used on his hands that morning. Shadow Man turned, his face eclipsed by the glare of the hall light. He saw Jones and fired, clipping Jones in the left arm, causing him to stumble and fall. Jones played dead. Shadow Man moved closer in order to finish him off, like Abrams, but Jones jumped up, swiftly knocking the gun to the floor with one hand and laying a punch into his cheekbones that swung his head to the side, blood spitting into the wall. Shadow Man recovered quickly and swung a punch directly into Jones' stomach, doubling him over, then rounded up with a punch to his jaw, sending him into the wall and unconscious. He reached down, out of breath, and picked up the gun, pointing it at Jones' head and pulling the trigger, but the mag was empty. He was about to finish Jones off in an alternative hands on fashion when he heard voices and saw guests rounding the corner, who proceeded to scream when they saw the two bodies on the floor and blood dripping down the wall. Shadow Man slipped the gun into his pocket, and walked quickly away from the screams as more feet came running to the scene. He opened the exit door, stepped outside, and disappeared.

Later, when Jones regained consciousness in the back of an ambulance, he knew that hadn't happened out the goodness of Shadow Man's heart. He never got a good look at his face, everything had happened so fast. No fingerprints were found on any item. He was a ghost. But even ghosts slip up and eventually show themselves, and

Jones would not give up until he found this Shadow Man.

The lift bounced to a stop, bringing Jones back to the present. The doors opened, and they exited the elevator, turned left, and knocked on room 419. Charlie asked the arranged questions behind the closed door. Cole answered. A thin camera then appeared under the door. Cole waved, and they all smiled. Charlie opened the door.

Miranda ran over, threw herself into Cole's arms, and started to sob. He comforted her, looking over to Trish, who nodded and came over and started to pat Miranda's back. "It's okay, Miranda, we're here now." Miranda stood up and took the tissue Trish handed her. Trish guided her over to the couch. "Who are these guys?" she asked, sniffling, pointing to Jones and 2Tall.

"I felt this needed to be handled properly, so I brought detectives Jones and Smith with me," Cole said.

Natalie walked over. Her eyes were swollen from crying, but she put on a strong face. It was clear she was no stranger to adversity. She extended her hand to Jones, then Smith. "Nice to meet you. Thank you for agreeing to help us. Shall we get started?"

Everyone took a seat.

"Ma'am," started Jones, "I'm not going to waste time, because we have to use it very carefully now. Do you know who the Shadow Man is?"

"Unless there is more than one, I believe it is my husband."

"We believe that as well, but we don't have proof. We have been tracking the Shadow Man for years now, but he has cleverly stayed hidden. He has been involved in drug deals, sex trafficking, and the list goes on. But we can't nail him, can't charge him, so can't convict him."

"Just recently," chimed in Smith, "the 16-year-old daughter of a Canadian military captain was taken by the Shadow Man's gang. They injected her with heroin—which they do to control their victims—and were prepared to then sell her for sex to the highest bidder."

Miranda started to cry, head in her hands.

"Fortunately, we received a tip and were able to rescue her before she was sold into the sex slave trade," Jones said. "She is now recovering in a Toronto hospital."

"But so many girls just don't get that lucky," said Smith.

"How could my father have done this? How? I can't believe it." Miranda started to cry again.

"We also got word that thirty girls were recently brought in from Moldova in a container. That is a long trek across the ocean, especially in a container. Shadow Man arranged that transaction. We believe those girls would have been sold as sex slaves for his profit. Luckily, they were rescued before that could happen and are now getting the care they deserve," said Smith.

"I've heard about this happening. But I didn't know these details. Sometimes I get a sanitized version in my job," said Natalie.

"Nothing sanitized about any of this," said Jones.

"What do you need me to do?" Natalie's voice was as hard and cold as the steel of a blade.

"I need you to get him to confess," Jones said.

"To what?"

"To his illegal activities. Primarily, the trafficking of girls. We will go over a list of questions. We need you to set up a meeting with him tonight."

"No way, that is too dangerous. He has hurt her before, and he'll do it again. No way." Miranda was standing now, her calm quickly being replaced by panic. Trish came over and gently led her back to the washroom, stopping at the bar fridge to grab a few mini bottles of vodka.

"She's not wrong," said Natalie. "He won't hesitate to hurt me. He put me in the hospital once before. And when he finds out I've opened the envelope, well, I don't think I'll be going to the hospital."

"We will be all around the building and can be inside within seconds," Smith said.

"It takes seconds to kill someone," she retorted.

"Do you really think he would do that?" Cole said.

"At this point, I'm not sure."

"I bet he wouldn't do it if Miranda was in the room," Trish said as she walked back out.

"She's too volatile, Trish, too young. No way," Smith said.

"I can do it," Miranda said. The vodka and the talk with Trish had refocused her.

"Are you sure, honey?" Natalie said.

"I am not letting you go in there alone, Mom."

"Actually, that may help," Jones said.

"Why?" Natalie asked.

"Because someone needs to wear a wire, a body pack as we call them, in order to convict Sokol. We need his words recorded. And you can't wear it, because you are his spouse."

"Nothing Sokol says would be admissible if he's talking to his wife," said Smith.

"Exactly," said Jones. "But Miranda can."

Everyone was silent.

"You want me to wear a wire? Record what he says?" Miranda whispered.

"It is the only way to put him away for good," Jones answered.

"If he finds it," Natalie swallowed, composing herself, "he'll kill her… and me."

Silence.

"Then we will just have to make sure he doesn't find it," Jones said.

"When will this happen?"

"This evening. In his office at the golf course," said Smith.

"We can watch that building and his office easily," said Jones. "We can keep an eye on you, and we will be listening and recording every word that is said. If we get even a hint that something is off, we will crash into that room so fast, he won't know what hit him," Jones said.

Natalie and Miranda joined hands and looked at each other.

"You okay with this, Miranda?"

"I'm not okay with any of it, but this needs to be done. So, yes. I'll do it."

"Okay. Well, in order for all of this to be above board and legal…"

"It can't be any other way or we won't get that bastard," Smith said.

"Exactly. So Miranda needs to be made an agent…"

"An agent? Like a secret agent?" said Miranda, her eyes popping open.

"Yes, a secret agent," said Jones. "It would only be for the one night."

"But that usually takes months," said Smith.

"Yes, normally, but as I work with CSO…"

"CSO?" Trish asked.

"Canadian Special Operations. It's an elite team for

situations just like this. And because of that, I have the federal prosecutor and the judge on speed-dial… she'll be an agent before we leave this room."

Everyone stopped and stared at each other. The gravity of the situation, the people involved, the amount at stake folded around them all like a landslide.

"Shall I make the call?" Jones said.

"Yes," said Miranda with an authority that surprised everyone, especially her mother. "Make the call."

EASTERN RIDGE GOLF AND COUNTRY CLUB, KINGSTON, ONTARIO, CANADA

It was a still, dark night. No wind. No moon. No stars. The clouds provided needed camouflage and a drizzle kind of rain. Jones, Trish, and 2Tall parked by the fairway off the first green in a Rogers Telecommunications van/surveillance vehicle. Their employees were always tinkering with lines and service. Tonight was as good as any for an outage. They sat and waited for Natalie to make her entrance. 2Tall looking through the sights of his sniper rifle directly into Sokol's office. If Cole couldn't get inside in time, he would finish Sokol with one shot. Cole sat in the truck on the road by the first green. He had a clear view into the large window of Sokol's office. Wearing a black slicker, boots, hat, and gloves, Bill sat in the bushes at the front of the clubhouse. Charlie was waiting back in the hotel room. They all wore coms.

At precisely 9:00 p.m. a car drove up and parked. "He's here," Bill alerted the rest of the team.

Sokol took his time getting into the building. Twenty minutes later, the second car showed up. Miranda and Natalie got out of the Tesla. "Birds have arrived," Bill said.

Cole could see the two women enter the office. Sokol was sitting in his chair, his back to the window. Natalie was in control; Miranda looked terrified. She could blow the whole thing right then and there. He spoke into her com. "Miranda, this is Cole. Just listen, don't react. Remember the twelfth hole at our tournament? You were unfocused and getting nervous. Stopped believing in your ability. You started hitting bad shots, and I came over and said, 'Pull yourself together, you're a professional, you can do this. Let's win.' Remember? Nod if you do." She nodded. "Good. This is an even bigger tournament. So pull yourself together. You can do this. Let's win." There was an instantaneous change in her demeanour. She stood taller. Her face calmed. Cole breathed a sigh of relief.

Sokol got up out of his chair. His voice was loud. Curt. Sharp. Razored. "You're late," he spat.

"I'm sorry, I ju—" Natalie.

"Shut up, you are fucking late. And what the hell is she doing here?"

"Dad, we came to talk with you, it ju—" She started to walk across the room to him, but as she came within arm's reach of him, his hand flashed forward and slapped her across the face. Her hand sprang to her cheek, tears stinging her eyes, thickening her resolve.

"Just sit down," he yelled. "Both of you, sit down."

They sat. Both were sweating and tense. "Calm," Jones said into their coms. "Stay calm. Focus on the plan. Stick to the script we rehearsed no matter what happens."

"Dad, I want to get a condo down in Florida, it's too

mu—"

"This is why you called me here?"

"Dad, we want to talk about this together. Just listen for a minute. I'm going to be down in Florida more often, and I don't just want to be in rentals or hotel rooms."

"So, why are we here?" he snapped.

"I thought we could help her with the purchase," said Natalie, "but I don't have enough in my account."

"So you want me to do it."

"Yes," Miranda and Natalie said together.

"Well, I don't have enough in my account either."

"Andrej, you know that isn't true. I just handed you an envelope the other day."

"Did you open that?" A dark cloud entered the room, his voice alarmingly quiet.

"Andrej, it doesn't take a rocket scientist to figure out there is money in those envelopes. Why can't we just give one to Miranda? There are dozens in there."

"Shut up, Natalie."

"Dozens of what?" Miranda asked.

"Doesn't matter."

"No, what envelopes? Dad?"

"From work, Miranda. Money from work, that's all."

"From the golf course?"

"None of your business."

"Well, maybe it *is* my business."

Sokol stood up so fast his chair flipped backward, crashing into the window; the whole wall shook. He clenched his fists.

Miranda stood up. "Dad, what is going on?" She feigned genuine shock well. Cole was impressed.

"Andrej, what *is* going on?" Natalie said.

"Did you open that envelope?" He was like a cobra waiting to attack.

Natalie was standing as well now. "Yes. Yes I did. How many girls, Andrej? How many girls? How many drugs? How could you?"

"What is she talking about? What girls?" Miranda was standing, her face still red from his slap, his fingers outlining her jawline.

Sokol started moving toward Natalie. "You broke our agreement," he hissed.

"You've broken everything," she spat back.

"WHAT GIRLS? WHAT GIRLS?" Miranda kept yelling this at Sokol until he lunged at her, grabbed her by the throat, and threw her to the floor. Miranda screamed.

"WHAT GIRLS, DAD? WHAT GIRLS?" Miranda kept yelling from the floor.

Sokol bent down, wrapped his hands around her neck, and started choking her. "Lots, Miranda. Lots of girls. Just as young and beautiful as you. I sell them like I sell drugs, okay? How do you think I've financed everything? This stupid golf course? I don't even fucking like golf. And I never liked you either. And now you're just a liability." His hands tightened around her neck, her lips turning blue. Natalie threw herself onto her husband, knocking him over. A shot blasted through the plate glass window, shattering it instantly, and Jones and Bill leaped in and over the glass. Bill dove onto Sokol, who was stronger than he thought. He had to wrestle to get him into a headlock so Jones could secure zip-ties on his wrists and ankles.

Once Sokol was subdued, Jones turned to the women, huddled together in a mass of shivering muscles and tears. He gently pulled them to their feet.

"Did you get what you needed?" asked Natalie.

"We sure did. You two were fantastic." He pulled them to their feet and guided them out the door to a waiting Cole.

"You okay?"

"Well, we're not dead," said Miranda, shaking like it was a subzero temperature in the room. She had really thought her dad was going to kill her. Not something she would ever forget.

"After this, I don't think anyone on the golf course is going to be able to intimidate you," said Cole. Miranda leaned into him. They walked to the front lobby and through the large oak doors where Smith was waiting to pick them up and take them back to the hotel.

As Cole opened the door to the Jeep, Miranda turned to him. "Thanks, Cole. Thanks so much." She hugged him and then climbed into the vehicle.

Natalie extended her hand. Cole shook it and smiled. Nothing more needed to be said. He closed the door and tapped the roof of the Jeep, then watched as it drove off. Trish came to stand beside Cole.

"They were great. Pretty gutsy," Trish said.

"Incredibly gutsy. Man, that Sokol. What a fucking prick."

"Yeah. Dollars to donuts the justice system will let us down on that one."

"Well, let's hope that's not true. God, would I like a piece of him."

Trish laughed. "I bet you would." She bumped his shoulder and smiled. "Did we get enough? Will the courts have enough?"

"Yeah, I think so. I hope so. And we have Misha, and we'll get Katya, so we have a lot of balls in our court. Plus, I recorded the whole convo as well, just in case the body pack wasn't functioning."

"Smart. Never know with those devices." Trish paused and looked down.

"What is it?"

"I didn't want to muddy the waters, but there's something I haven't told you."

"What is it?"

"The skinny guy was shot in the head when I went over to check on them."

"You've got to be fucking kidding me."

"Wish I was."

"Misha?"

"Gone."

"How?"

"I"m guessing Katya."

"Where's the body?"

"In the back of my Jeep."

"You've been driving around with a dead body in the vehicle?"

"Well, yeah. I mean, what was I supposed to do?"

Cole laughed. "We'll see what Jones wants to do with it."

"Good, because I could use a little help. Dead bodies are heavy. Hurt my back a bit." They laughed. "Let's go and see if Jones needs any help."

"We'll have to tell him about Misha," said Cole. "Katya and Misha are Sokol's backbone. But their minions are probably more than we could track."

"Well, let's concentrate on what we have now, the big fish." They walked back inside, down the hall to the office. Sokol was sitting in a chair, zip-tied.

Jones pulled him up. "Let's go."

"You have nothing on me."

"That's where you're wrong, my friend. Everything you just said was recorded. And don't think I have forgotten that I saw you kill Abrams in the Caymans. We have you and now…" Sokol watched, his eyes widening by the second, as Bill pressed the button under the desk and opened the chamber door, then walked in with his arms wide. "We have your whole operation, complete with data bases and code books." Jones smiled, almost wickedly.

"I destroyed that book."

"But not the photos we took of it first," Bill said.

Sokol blanched. "I should have fucking killed you when I had the chance. It's not the end."

"It is for you," Jones said.

PEARSON INTERNATIONAL AIRPORT, TORONTO, ONTARIO, CANADA

The woman hired to impersonate Katya presented her ticket to the airline agent, as well as her passport, and walked down the jetway to board Boeing 787 bound for Europe. She stowed her bag securely in the bin over her seat, settled herself into the window seat, and snugged up her seatbelt. She took a deep breath. Payment had been wired to her account in the Czech Republic. She put her head back and closed her eyes. Easy money.

A Red Notice had been issued worldwide for Katya's arrest, and Interpol had been put on alert. They would soon be highly disappointed.

NEAR BROCKVILLE, ONTARIO, CANADA

Beeping machines and the hum of the ventilation system surrounded the ten girls lying in hospital beds. They were all sedated and hooked up to IV drips. Nurses monitored them regularly, and a guard was posted outside the room.

"How are they doing?" Constable Stokely asked as the nurse walked into the hall. She was one of the officers that had rescued the girls from the white vans; nurses were more than happy to give her information.

"They are stable. Which is a good start."

"Were they able to shower, get some clean clothes?"

"Yes, with assistance. All their clothes were disposed of and there are clothing donations coming in from so many people."

"Are these girls hooked up to the machines in critical shape?"

"Serious, but not critical. It would have been critical if they had not been rescued when they were."

"Why are only ten here?"

"The others weathered the storm better, I guess. Everyone is different. For these girls, the dehydration and high cortisol levels became too much for them. Let's be grateful you got them before they started 'working.'" She shook her head with a strained look on her face.

"Yes. Often that's when we bring them here in body bags."

The nurse looked up with wide eyes. The constable met her gaze.

"Well, let's be glad that didn't happen this time," said the nurse. "How long will you be posted here?"

"We want to be sure there isn't a threat of retaliation. Probably until they're moved."

"To where the other girls went at Covenant House?"

"Yes."

They stood in silence as an orderly wheeled a stretcher past them.

"Will they get protection at the other facility as well?" asked the nurse.

"Yes. We will do our best."

A machine started beeping in the room where the girls were and the nurse turned to leave. The constable leaned against the wall. She pulled out her phone, dialled the number of the cop at Covenant House, and put the phone to her ear. "Hi, just checking in. How are the girls doing over there?"

"Super quiet. Grateful. Little Adela is quite something. She's translating all over the place, and we have already made contact with a few families."

"When my shift if done here, I'll pop over."

"Great. We're a bit short staffed."

"I know. Are they talking yet?"

"Minimally. The food and water is helping, of course. They need sleep. They are seriously traumatized."

"Okay. Hopefully they can start to help us put together the pieces. Have Europol and Frontex been alerted?" Stokely asked.

"Yes. They've also been alerted that Sokol is now in custody, in case they have any outstanding warrants for him. Fucking bastard."

"Is he still sitting in that holding cell?"

"Yeah, but they're transferring him later today. Too bad it's not to the cemetery."

"That would be letting him off too easy."

"Yeah. Maybe. Anyway, I have to get back."

"Okay. See you later," Stokely said and hung up.

She smiled at the nurses as she walked down the hall. "Just getting a coffee," she called to them. The elevator was empty as she stepped inside. She pulled out her private phone as the doors closed behind her. Her call was answered on the first ring.

"Get the van ready and the two guys armed. Tell them to meet me at the junction in fifteen minutes. Sharp. That's job one. Make it happen. We have two jobs that can't wait. And I'm not messing around. Job two: forget the girls at the hospital, they'll be no good to us. The others will recover. No, they're at Covenant House. Listen, we didn't spend all this money to let these girls go free, they need to make us some cash. Decide who will best get those girls back and take them to our regular house. It hasn't been compromised. We'll nurse them back to health ourselves and then put them to work as planned. And Misha, you have to finish Natalie and Miranda. They'll be at a wedding tomorrow. Don't fuck this up. Sokol and I will be gone for a while, but not forever. Get it done, or you will be the one with a bullet in your head."

PETERBOROUGH, ONTARIO, CANADA

Captain Jim Morrison sat at the dining room table with his mom and dad and two daughters. They were playing Scrabble.

"No way, Dad, you can't do that, it's not even a word," Abby said.

"It's a word I use."

"Not a word anyone else uses," said Grammy Morrison.

"Fine. I'll just do this." He put two tiles on the board.

"*IS*. That's the best you can do?" Abby said.

"Unless you want to help me out here."

"No helping," Abby said. "Good for you to lose once in a while, Dad."

"Once in a while? I never win this game."

"Not with words like *IS* you won't," said Grandpa Morrison.

They all laughed. Everyone was enjoying the fact that Jim was actually home for more than a day or two and that Hailey was starting to talk and smile again. Her friends had come over for a visit, but they knew for a while there would always be an adult in the room. Emotions were still precarious, and conversations needed to be monitored. The therapist had been very clear about strategies going forward. No one disagreed. Especially Hailey. She was well aware that she had been lucky, so very lucky.

Mac walked into the room, bringing bowls of chips and pretzels. She put them on the table and scrutinized the board. "*IS*? Was that Jim?" Jim put his head into his hands as everyone laughed. "Jim, got a minute?"

"We'll call you when it's your turn again, Dad," said Abby.

Jim got up and followed Mac into the kitchen. She had come to visit and check up on Hailey and Jim.

"New info?" asked Jim.

"Yes. They rescued the other girls."

"How many?"

"Thirty."

Jim shook his head and took a deep breath. "And Shadow Man?"

"They got him."

"Well, at least that's one down."

"Yeah. Hajek is still out there, but police are hoping with Shadow Man in custody, he'll talk."

"Not likely, fucking bastards."

"How's she doing, honestly?"

"She's not the same girl. Quiet. Cautious. Cries a lot. Hard to watch. Breaks my heart I wasn't there to stop it all."

"Don't do that to yourself. It hasn't been long, Jim. Give her some time. And give yourself some time. This wasn't your fault."

"I know. I know."

"You staying for a while?"

"I've taken an indefinite leave. Kinda feel I need to be here until she finds some kind of balance. Can't leave that to Mom and Dad."

"No, you can't. Good call."

"What's happening with the other girls?"

"Most have been released from the hospital. A few are now in critical condition, but most are doing well. Covenant House is so amazing. Cole also managed to get them some financial help. Sokol's wife Natalie offered. The girls will have their trip paid for to get home, and each will have a good sum of money to help them get on their feet."

"Wow. That's great."

"Natalie felt it was the least she could do. I think she's also trying to set up a government task force." She gave Jim a sideways glance.

"Really?"

"I think you would be perfect. Give you something to do. I gave her your contact info."

"Thanks, Mac. I would love to do that. But it may not be so easy for her to get things done right now. Have you seen the news?

"Not in the last six hours. Why?"

"It's everywhere," said Jim. "That a minister in the

cabinet was married to a gang leader. They're screaming for her resignation."

"Yeah, I did hear that. I'm not surprised. But she didn't know he was in the mob, to be fair."

"Maybe not, but maybe she just didn't want to see the signs."

"That is true," said Mac. "I mean those envelopes should have been a start. But she was afraid. Fear can paralyze."

"We've both seen that time and again in our line of work."

"She wants to make amends, I hope they let her. But frankly, she's going to have to resign her post, and maybe her position as MP too."

"Well, she may have to create the task force as a citizen."

"Maybe, but not right now, there's a lot of shit about to hit the fan. I really wouldn't want to be in her shoes right now." They paused, taking some deep breaths. It was a lot to process.

"Will you be still coming to visit now and again?" asked Jim.

"Try and keep me away. Don't want you going stir-crazy."

"Well, I'm thinking of starting a hobby."

"From the looks of things, I hope it's not Scrabble."

She playfully punched him in the arm and he pulled her into a hug.

"Why don't we all drive down together for the wedding?" Mac suggested.

"I was just thinking the same thing."

"Okay, well, we'll discuss all the logistics later."

"Daaadd," called Abby. "Your turn!"

"I think you have a game to lose," said Mac.

"Guess that's my cue," said Jim.

Mac smiled and patted him on the shoulder. "Try for some words with more than two letters this time." She nudged him, and he smiled. "It's going to be okay, Jim."

Jim looked at his family in the other room and was filled with a warmth. "Yeah, I know."

POLICE STATION, KINGSTON, ONTARIO, CANADA

At 3:30 p.m. a van pulled up at the side entrance of the Kingston Police Station. Constable Stokely got out and walked to the side door, punching in her code. She approached the desk.

"That scumbag Sokol ready for transfer?" she asked.

"The transfer time I have is 4:00 p.m."

"Yeah, well I got finished at the hospital a bit early, so thought I'd take him off your hands."

"Yeah, sure. I'll just let the provincial jail know you're on your way. We have two guards that will accompany you."

"Good. I'm just outside in the unmarked transport van. The guards can load him in from the back."

"Copy that." He picked up the phone to alert the guards to prepare Sokol for transport. Stokely walked back out to the van and waited in the driver's seat.

When the guards exited the building with Sokol in handcuffs and leg shackles, she quietly nodded as they looked at her through the window. They proceeded to the back of the van. Each guard opened a door. Within seconds, bullets from two silenced guns penetrated the chest of each guard. The shooters lunged forward and dragged them into the van, Sokol stepped over the bodies and into the vehicle, and sat on the bench. The doors were pulled closed and the van pulled away.

Around two corners was an underground parking garage. The van pulled into the garage and drove to the far corner. The shooters got out carrying hand tools and took off each license plate, replacing them with a new one, then put decals on the side of the van that read *Telecommunications*. They pulled out the dead bodies, put them in garbage bags, and left them in the garage. They then cut off the shackles and handcuffs Sokol was wearing, handing him a pair of jeans, a blue t-shirt, and a hoodie. He changed quickly and jumped into the passenger seat up front. Stokely had already changed into jeans and a green sweatshirt with *Nike* written on the front. She put on her New York Yankees cap.

"Good to see you, Katya," said Sokol.

"Didn't think I'd just leave you in there, did you?"

"Wasn't sure." He smiled at her. "Who are the guys in the back?"

"Our hired guns. I'll get rid of them when we change vehicles. We'll be safe when we cross the border."

"American?"

"Mexican."

"And the girls?" asked Sokol.

"It's being taken care of. While we lie low, they'll be nursed back to health and be ready to work as soon as we are. I have guys in charge."

"And Natalie and Miranda?"

"They should be keeping those guys in the garbage bags company very soon."

"Who's doing that?"

"Misha." Katya kept her eyes on the road.

Sokol drew in a long breath, whistling out between his teeth. "Excellent. I'm dying for a coffee.

EASTERN RIDGE GOLF AND COUNTRY CLUB, KINGSTON, ONTARIO, CANADA

It wasn't long after that memorable dinner at Cynthia's favourite restaurant that Charlie decided to pop the question. He had kept it quiet from the team because so much was happening. But after Sokol's arrest, it seemed the right time to add even more joy. Everyone was thrilled. As they had waited long enough, the wedding was planned for the next week, and Natalie had offered the golf course.

A tall, white arbor, wide enough for three people to stand under, had been erected at the edge of the patio amongst the clay pots of petunias, geraniums, and impatiens. Roses and lilies and daisies were woven in and out of the white latticed arbor. Petals from the same flowers were scattered throughout the groups of chairs set up in rows, all gazing toward the arbor. The warm sun sparkled off the koi pond to the side of the patio as it gently bubbled and trickled water around lilies and goldfish. Gentle breezes carried summer bird songs, accompanied by a string quartet. People meandered carrying flutes of champagne while the silk fabrics of warmly coloured dresses and elegant dark tux tails swooshed festively.

After more than twenty years, Cynthia and Charlie were finally tying the knot.

Miranda wore a short emerald green dress with a

plunging back. She was immersed in conversation with some of Cynthia's friends. Natalie was circulating, watching the festivities, her security detail never far behind. She had begun to receive threats once the news of Sokol hit the press. But she was determined to make sure this day was sparkling, everyone certainly needed some sparkle. She looked elegant in her soft rose pantsuit.

Jones had wanted to put Miranda and Natalie into a witness protection program until Sokol and Hajek were behind maximum security bars, but she had resisted. She knew she had to step down as minister of justice, which broke her heart. And she accepted that she would also resign as a member of parliament. She decided on a new career, one aligned with her daughter: she decided to try her hand at running the Eastern Ridge golf course. It would be a different kind of life, and she was ready for that. Instead of witness protection, Jones had put in place an executive protection team, plain clothes agents that would watch Natalie and Miranda's every move, wherever they were, until they were deemed out of danger… which could prove to be a rather long time.

Cole, handsome in his tuxedo, had Mac on his arm. She was dressed in a deep mauve gown. They hadn't been on a night out together in too long.

"Aren't you a sight," said Jim Morrison as he came to stand beside Mac. He planted a kiss on her cheek. "Cole," he extended his hand, "I never got to formally thank you for saving my daughter."

Cole nodded in acknowledgement. "Thanks Jim. I'm glad we were able to make things happen. Hi Hailey, I'm so glad to see you feeling better."

"Certainly better than the last time you saw me."

Cole laughed. "Well, if she can joke about it, she's doing great."

"She takes after me like that," said Jim, pulling Hailey into a bear hug.

"This must be Abby, and Grandpa and Grammy Morrison," Cole said, extending his hand. "So nice to meet you all. And so glad you could be here today with all of us to celebrate!"

"Yes, we all need a little celebration to balance out the last few months," said Grandpa Morrison.

"Hailey is looking a little tired," said Grammy Morrison, adjusting the floral patterned silk scarf that adorned her dress. "Let's go and find our seats, dear." She took Hailey's hand and together they walked toward the chairs, smiling at Jim as they left. Abby joined them.

"Mom always did have great timing," said Jim.

"Seriously, Jim, how is she doing?" asked Cole.

"Seriously? Okay, but she has a long way to go. She's afraid to be on her own. One of us has to be with her all the time. It's hard to get her to eat. She can't forgive herself for choices she made. The list goes on and on. Seriously? It's fucking hard."

"You're home now. Things will get better, Jim," said Mac. "I mean, even a couple of weeks ago she wouldn't have been able to come to a big event like this, so she's making progress. Slow and steady. She'll get there."

"I hope so," said Jim. "At least you got that bastard. I heard Charlie even has a finger in one of his jars. That made me feel a hell of a lot better." They all smiled.

"Yes, fingers and jars, redemption at its best." Cole laughed.

Trish saw Cole across the patio and waved. He gestured for her to come over.

"Well, look who the cat dragged in," said Jim as he pulled Trish into a bear hug. "Great to see you, and under much better circumstances. But I'll get involved in a barroom brawl with you any day."

"Back atcha big guy. It was nice we could work together, Jim," said Trish.

"I'll catch up with you guys a bit later. Going to go and sit with my family. Damn, it's nice to say that." And he walked toward the chairs with a smile on his face.

"Don't you look stunning," Mac said to Trish, who sparkled in her pale yellow outfit. They leaned in and hugged.

"This old thing?" Trish winked and moved to hug

Cole. "Did you ever think you'd see this day? I mean, Charlie. Finally."

"Honestly? No. But I couldn't be more thrilled," said Cole.

"I'm surprised to see Kitch here," said Mac.

"Oh, come on, you know my dad wouldn't miss this. They've been friends for years," said Cole.

"Yeah, even left his dream vacation to be here," said Bill as he sauntered into the conversation.

"You eavesdropping on our convo, Bill?" asked Mac.

"Damn right I am," said Bill. "Man, Kitch looks good. Great he could make it."

"Yeah, I'm glad he's here too," said Trish.

"It wasn't by accident," said Cole.

"Why doesn't that surprise me?" said Bill.

"When this all went into motion, Charlie had said that he wished Kitch was around because he really wanted him to be his best man. So, I made a few calls. Call it my wedding gift."

"Perfect gift," said Mac.

"What gift?" asked 2Tall as he waltzed over.

"That Kitch is here as Charlie's best man," said Trish.

"Wow, that's pretty awesome."

"By the way, you are still Mr. Smith, and Bill, you're a buddy from golfing long ago. Charlie's story holds up because he was on detail. We need to keep our covers intact," said Cole.

"Does Natalie know about all that with Cynthia?" asked 2Tall.

"Not sure, and I'm not going to be the one to bring it up," said Cole. "I'm sure it will all come out in the wash."

"Speak of the devil," said Trish. They all quickly smiled and changed the subject.

"Cole, Trish, so glad you're both here," said Natalie. "When Charlie had mentioned that he was looking for a venue for his wedding, I jumped at the chance. I mean, we need some new vibes around here." Natalie widened her eyes, and everyone nodded in agreement. "Miranda was so excited to do this. Where is she?"

"She's over chatting with some new friends." Trish pointed.

"She needs some fun," said Natalie. "It's all been pretty shocking."

"Yes, it's a lot to take in for sure," Cole said.

"It's all really beautiful, Natalie. You've done a spectacular job for the wedding. Certainly is transformed from when we're here playing golf," said Trish.

"Thanks. We wanted it to be special. It's really the least I could do," said Natalie. "And you are...?" She reached over to shake Mac's hand.

"Oh, I'm so sorry. This is Mac," said Cole.

"So nice to meet you. Do you follow Cole on tour?" asked Natalie.

"As much as possible, yes," said Mac, keeping a very straight face.

"Mr. Smith, so nice you could come. I'm so indebted to all of you," said Natalie.

"We did make quite the team," said Jones as he joined the group.

"Sergeant Jones, thank you so much, again," said Natalie.

"It is you I should be thanking," said Jones. "Without your courage none of this would have happened."

Natalie smiled and warmly hugged him. "Now to the reason we are all here. I see the minister waving to me, so I think that means we all need to take our seats." Natalie waved to Miranda who walked over so they could sit together. Natalie put her arm around her daughter and looked toward the seating, choosing her spot.

At the same time, Cole got a chill down his spine. He grabbed 2Tall's arm who was standing beside him, and pulled his ear close. "I'm not sure what's going on, but something bad is about to happen. I just know it. I can't do anything about it. Get your weapon ready."

2Tall slid his hand underneath his jacket, pulling his weapon out of the holster and into the ready position. His eyes scanned the area without his head moving. Bill moved to stand beside Cole. He leaned in and whispered, "We have a problem. See that waiter over there," he nodded his head and Cole and 2tall turned to look. "It's Misha. Sokol's right hand."

"Fuck," said Cole. "Bill, alert Jones. 2Tall, go and stand with Natalie and Miranda, get the security details attention. They're here for those two women."

The minister stood waiting under the arbor. Guests were all taking their places. But Misha saw Bill and dropped his tray, pulling out his weapon. At the same time, Bill yelled and 2Tall pulled Miranda and Natalie to the ground as shots were fired. People started screaming and crouching; one of the bullet's grazed Abby's shoulder; blood starting running down her arm. She looked up at her dad in shock. Jim went into attack mode. He scanned the area for the shooter, saw him, and starting running toward him. 2Tall held up his gun and Jim grabbed it as he ran past him. Misha held his weapon, pointing it straight at Jim, but Jim was too fast. He fired and put a bullet in Misha's head and chest. The security team was right behind him, and they quickly dealt with the body. Mac had worked quickly, wrapping Grammy Morrison's scarf around Abby's shoulder. Jim came running back, out of breath, flushed.

"Is she okay?"

"She's okay," said Mac. "It's just a flesh wound."

"I'm okay, Dad. Let's just sit down for a minute."

Everyone was shaken. Kitch was talking quietly to Charlie and then stood back and addressed the guests.

"What an awful event we have all just witnessed. I trust everyone is okay. My dear friend Charlie here would like to marry the love of his life. If everyone agrees we should continue, please raise your hands."

There was a cheer from the crowd and everyone started clapping. Charlie smiled and moved to stand beside the minister. Kitch moved beside Charlie, and Cynthia's sister, the maid of honour, waited on the opposite side of the arbor. The string quartet began, and everyone turned to look behind them. Cynthia, on the arm of her father, began to walk down the aisle; her train softly flowed behind her beautifully scalloped wedding dress, pearl buttons all down the back. She wore daisies in her hair and long snowdrop earrings. She was beautiful. She took her place beside Charlie, who wrapped her hand around his arm, his face a beacon of sunlight.

It was a simple, touching ceremony, and when they kissed there was a cheer from the crowd. After the bride tossed her bouquet, caught by a blushing Trish, everyone was handed a glass of champagne with a small strawberry at the bottom. The bleeding had stopped in Abby's shoulder and she happily accepted the flute of champagne. She looked over at her dad, lifting up the glass. "You don't mind?"

"Mind? I'd say it's imperative." He leaned over and kissed her on the cheek. "You were amazing."

"I had a good teacher," she smiled up at him.

"Come on," he said. "Let's get you into the clubhouse and get a real dressing for that arm. Maybe after today my daughters could just lay low for a while."

Bill joined Jim and Abby as they walked to the clubhouse. "Impressive, Jim." He clapped him on the back.

"I just couldn't help myself," said Jim. "He was the guy from the bar. I recognized him. They already messed with one of my daughters, I wasn't going wait to see what happened."

"You did good, man."

"Thanks Bill. I'm going to get this one some medical attention now."

Jones and 2Tall were talking with Natalie and Miranda. "You okay? No injuries?" asked Jones.

"No, we're okay," said Natalie. "A bit shaken, but okay. I am glad they finished the wedding. That would have just been awful."

"I recognized the waiter," said Miranda. "He worked for Dad."

"Yes," said Jones. "Yes, he did."

"Well, guess we won't have any more problems from him," said Natalie, and everyone burst into nervous laughter.

"Stay close to your security guys for a while," said 2Tall.

"Yes, we absolutely will," said Natalie.

"I'm glad to hear that," said Jones.

"Shall we get some more champagne?" asked Miranda.

"I thought you'd never ask," said Jones, smiling.

Charlie and Cynthia were signing papers. "Will being married to you always be this exciting?" asked Cynthia.

Charlie leaned over and kissed his bride. "Absofuckinglutely," he said.

"He was one of the guys from all those years ago, wasn't he?" asked Cynthia.

"Yeah, yes he was," said Charlie.

"So we've got them all now."

"We do. Now, it's our turn." This time, she leaned in to kiss him. He took her face between his hands and kissed her right on the lips.

Cole wasn't used to being a bystander when shit went down. He sipped his champagne and took a deep breath. He was proud of his team; and Jim, well, Jim was a father scorned. Cole felt a tap on his shoulder. He knew that tap, and the realization of who was doing the tapping did not warm his heart. When he turned around, he felt his body stand to attention.

"Poison," Cole said.

"Buckman."

"I assume this is not a social visit. Even though it is a wedding."

"No."

"And?"

"And there are plane tickets on *Windy Girl* for you and your team of Wookies. I expect to see all of you in my office on the other side of the pond end of the week. The itinerary is also with the tickets."

"You couldn't have called?"

"And miss seeing the look on your face? Not a chance. Plus, it was a wedding no one will ever forget! See you at the end of the week." She emptied her champagne flute, handing it to Cole.

The Wookies, having witnessed the interaction, slowly made their way to Cole.

"What's Poison doing here?" Bill asked.

"Guess we will find out end of the week. Apparently she left tickets for us on *Windy Girl*."

"And how did she…" Bill stopped himself. "Yup, sounds about right."

"Are we going somewhere?" Trish asked.

"We are. But don't ask me anything, because I have no answers at present." Cole laughed.

"What about Charlie and his honeymoon?" 2Tall asked.

"Well, he has the rest of this week. Besides, I'm sure Charlie would love some British fingers to fill some of his jars."

They all laughed as Charlie walked in their direction. They hugged him, one by one.

"Congrats, man," said Bill.

"So happy for you, Charlie," Trish added.

"Well, no one will say this was a boring wedding," said Charlie. Everyone laughed.

"Itchy for a few European fingers, Charlie?" Cole asked.

"What do you mean?"

"We are flying to Britain on a mission end of the week."

"Is that my honeymoon?"

"Interesting you should ask that."

They all stood, smiling, watching the birds fly overhead.

Cole saw Jones approaching out of the corner of his eye. He came and stood beside Cole and whispered, "I need a word. In private."

Cole's face didn't change as he turned and walked away with Jones.

"What's happening?"

"Sokol's gone."

"What the fuck? First Misha, now you tell me Sokol's escaped? How?"

"Not sure of the details yet, but two guards were found dead in an underground garage near the jail. And the license plates from the vehicle videotaped outside the police station… they were lying beside the bodies."

"Holy fuck."

"The video camera showed a female driving the van away. Constable Stokely." Jones paused for effect.

"Let me guess. Katya. Sokol's sidekick."

"Yup."

Cole took in a deep breath and glanced over to the jovial wedding party. "Time to work outside the box."

"Want me to get a team together?"

"No. This will just be me and Sokol. I'm putting an end to this myself."

"Want me to assist?"

"No. We started this, we'll finish it, the Wookie way."

"Cole, it's dangerous. *They're* dangerous."

"That's my flavour, Jones."

Trish was looking in Cole's direction. He waved her over, 2Tall and Bill were not too far behind. They were all standing together, sipping champagne.

"What's up?" Bill asked.

"Brace yourselves."

"Sokol's gone," Jones said.

Trish almost dropped her glass. 2Tall spat out the Champagne in his mouth.

"What the fuck?" Bill said.

"My thoughts exactly," said Jones.

"When do we leave?" 2Tall said.

"We don't," said Cole. "I do."

"WHAT?" they all said in unison.

"This is a one-person job, in and out. But I need my Wookies."

"Of course you do," Bill said.

"So, here's what we're going to do. Trish and Bill, you are going track and find this bastard. He's with Katya."

"Did she spring him?" 2Tall asked.

"She did. As Constable Stokely."

"You're fucking kidding me." 2Tall shook his head.

"Wish he was," said Jones.

"The way I see it, they are likely heading to Mexico," Cole said.

"And they won't be flying," Trish added.

"Right. So they'll be switching vehicles and will take the shortest route," Jones said.

"Probably through Toronto to Cleveland, Indiana, Memphis, and Texas to the border," said Trish.

"So because of our time frame…" Cole said.

"We need to grab them before they cross that Mexican border," 2Tall finished.

"Time-wise, Indiana makes the most sense," Bill suggested.

"They'll have to sleep there. Will probably drive straight through," Jones said.

"I'll book you a flight to Indiana."

"Not a word to Charlie," Cole warned. Everyone nodded. "We'll say our goodbyes and say Poison has some work for us."

"We'll head over to *Windy Girl* and get started," 2Tall said.

"I'll keep mingling here. Want a word with the security detail before I leave. Cole, keep me posted," Jones said. Cole nodded.

"Okay. I'm heading to the airport. Let's get this bastard, once and for all."

INDIANAPOLIS, INDIANA, U.S.A.

Cole hadn't wasted a minute; neither had the Wookies. Through contacts, video tracking in various states, facial recognition, and Internet sleuthing, Trish and Bill found Sokol and Katya. They were driving a silver Ford Taurus after dumping the van and were parked outside a Motel 6, just south of Interstate 465, in Indianapolis, Indiana.

Once Cole's flight landed in Indianapolis, he rented a white Hyundai Santa Fe and headed for 500 Guns, the best gun shop in the area; he needed firepower. 2Tall had called ahead, making sure the exact weapons would be waiting and paid for, along with dark jeans and a black hoodie. Cole made good time, parked outside, and walked into the shop. He showed his ID, and the guy handed him two Glock 23 handguns, threaded barrel and suppressor, and Winchester Ranger 40S&W bullets, 180 grain hollow-points, loaded.

"That is some serious firepower you're packing there, man," said the clerk. "Hope you're gonna be ready for the kickback when you pull that trigger. I seriously don't wanna know what you're shootin'."

"That's good you're not asking," said Cole as he collected his supplies and headed out to the rented vehicle. He stowed the gear in the back seat and drove around the corner to where he saw a Denny's; he needed a coffee and a tuna sandwich for the drive over to Motel 6.

Dusk was settling around his vehicle as he pulled into the driveway beside the motel. He finished his sandwich, emptied his coffee cup, and pulled out his binoculars. Sure as shit, there sat the silver Ford Taurus outside room 112. They'd be tired from the adrenaline and the long drive. He figured they'd be sound asleep as the Big Dipper started twinkling above. Cole leaned his seat back. He knew how to be patient, conserve energy, and wait for the moment.

He meant this to be slick and quick. Standard take-out mission. They didn't know he was coming. No one would even know he'd ever been there. It was his specialty, or one of them, anyway. When the clock struck midnight, he pulled up the hood of his black sweatshirt, stepped out of his vehicle, and disappeared into the moonless night. He adjusted the silencers on his two Glocks, one in his left hand, one in his belt, and then he checked the knife against his leg.

Staying close to walls and buildings, he made his way down to room 112. The only sound was the buzz of the vending machine at the end of the row of rooms and the dull sound of traffic in the distance. He didn't want to bust down the door, didn't want to draw any attention. He pulled out his phone, on which Trish had placed an app to silently enter the room without a key card. The door clicked. He waited. And waited again. No additional sound. He counted to three, took a breath, and slowly turned the handle on the door, stepped inside gingerly, and pulled the door closed behind him.

The room was pitch dark, punctuated by snorts of snoring, one in each bed. He moved to the space between the beds, secured the Glock with both hands, and kicked the bed. He wanted to be sure it was Sokol and Katya. The one body groaned and rolled over: Sokol. Then the other: Katya. The whites of their eyes glowed in the dark room. "This is the end of the road, Sokol," said Cole and shot him in the head, then turned and double-tapped Katya as she was reaching under her pillow for her weapon.

Cole turned and quietly opened the door, stepped into the night air, silently closing it behind him. He stood for a moment looking left and right. And then without a sound, he walked back to his waiting Santa Fe.

Driving down the road, he called Trish. "Targets are neutralized. I'll see all you sweethearts at the airport in a few days. Wookies have some work across the pond. And let my girl know I'll meet her at our spot in eight hours."

"Copy that." She smiled as she hung up, turning to give a thumbs up to Bill and 2Tall sitting across the room. Bill opened the fridge and pulled out three beers, popping the lids off and handing them around. They all clicked and then gratefully drank.

Could working across the pond be half as exciting as this? They were about to find out.

POSTSCRIPT

Thousands of girls are sold into sex slavery every year, more commonly known as human trafficking, all over the world. Canada is no exception. These are girls and young women ranging in age from 13 to 25. They can be grabbed at parties, clubs, convinced online, approached at work, offered jobs for cleaning or secretarial work, only to find themselves locked into containers and shipped to another country. They are told that if they don't cooperate their families will be in danger. They are often forced to use drugs in order to keep them compliant. Their lives are at serious risk. The people who engage in these sexual activities need to be brought to justice, but the girls need to be saved first. If you have a suspicion about a girl you have seen or know, please don't hesitate to reach out to:

CanadianHumanTraffickingHotline.ca

Canadian Human Trafficking Hotline - 1-833-900-1010

publicsafety.gc.ca

covenanthousetoronto.ca

In the United States of America call 1-888-373-7888

Or email help@humantraffickinghotline.org

In a text type HELP and send it to 233733 (BEFREE)

Also, ourrescue.org can help.

PUT A STOP TO HUMAN TRAFFICKING/
SEX SLAVERY!

ACKNOWLEDGEMENTS

Don and I would like to thank Alanna at Chicken House Press for giving Cole Buckman the chance to be read; Alister Thompson for editing with an edge; Mitch Reed for your fantastic observations and support; Lynne Brophy for your insight and brainstorming afternoons; Matt Ysinga, we couldn't have done this without you; to our families and friends for their constant encouragement and to all the first responders out there who put their lives on the line for us every day in trying to make our world a better place. And thank you to all our readers!

Marina L. Reed

ABOUT THE AUTHOR/CREATORS

Marina has lived and worked around the world as a journalist, educator, and artist. She is the author of twelve books, freelance articles, online workshops and television current affairs programs. She believes in the empowerment of individuals. Marina is currently working on her next novel.

Don served for over 30 years with a large Canadian Police Service, coming in direct contact with many homicide investigations. As a Detective Staff Sergeant, he specialized in International Security Operations. He is currently based in Toronto where he owns and operates a Security Consulting Firm.

Look for the new Cole Buckman novel,
Death at the Yellow Briar,
coming soon from Chicken House Press.

Send Marina your thoughts and comments.
instagram.com/marinalreed